Rhoda Broughton

Mrs. Bligh

A Novel

Rhoda Broughton

Mrs. Bligh
A Novel

ISBN/EAN: 9783337032722

Printed in Europe, USA, Canada, Australia, Japan

Cover: Foto ©Andreas Hilbeck / pixelio.de

More available books at **www.hansebooks.com**

MRS. BLIGH

A Novel

BY

RHODA BROUGHTON

AUTHOR OF
'COMETH UP AS A FLOWER,' 'DOCTOR CUPID,' 'ALAS!' ETC.

LONDON
RICHARD BENTLEY AND SON
Publishers in Ordinary to Her Majesty the Queen
1892

TO

ANDREW LANG,

THIS SLENDER STORY

IS OFFERED BY

THE AUTHOR.

MRS. BLIGH

CHAPTER I.

THE portals of that as unhandsome as highly-frequented place of worship, Holy Trinity Church, Chelsea, have just let loose the customary crowd of well-fed, well-to-do attendants on the 11.30 Sunday service. Their ears, and let us hope their hearts too, have been receiving the unsparing rebukes and virile admonishments weekly administered to them by the incumbent. It is doubtful whether the spirit of all the encomiums lavished on him by his furred and feathered flock as they stream home to their excellent luncheons this sharp-breathed Lenten Sunday would please him.

"He was finer than ever to-day!" says a mother to her daughter, in that tone of æsthetic relish that might have applauded the manner in which a popular actor has given a famous point, or a favourite soprano taken a high note; "I think it is the best series we have ever had; it outdoes the Beatitudes last year."

"I like the Beatitudes best still," replies the daughter, "but"—enthusiastically—"he certainly is A 1. I tried to catch your eye when he made that unmistakable allusion to baccarat. I wonder how Lord —— felt! It is so annoying that we sit behind him, and so could not see his face. I noticed that he bent his head quite low down."

"I expect a good many people have come out not feeling very comfortable," replies the parent, with a complacency which shows that she has no apprehension of belonging to that distempered band, and in the same spirit of confident superiority which dictated Totty

Poyser's speech about her brothers: "Dey naughty naughty boys! *me* dood."

"Mrs. Bligh has gone out of mourning!" cries the girl, with that admirably abrupt change of idea for which the female mind has a special aptitude; and indicating a middle-sized woman, who is lightly and alone walking homewards ahead of them. "I knew what it meant when she broke out into an eruption of Parma violets on Septuagesima Sunday."

"She has something yellow about her, has not she? Dear me, how bad my eyes are!"

"She has planted a mimosa bush in her bonnet: she is determined that there shall be no mistake about her being out of mourning. I fancy"—uncharitably—"that *inside* she has been out of mourning some time."

"Poor woman, one cannot blame her! It would have been rank hypocrisy in her to have pretended it was anything but a happy release; and I hear that, in spite of her mimosa, she has a perfect horror of a second venture. Ah, Mr. Blank" (to a beautifully-clad young gentleman who now joins them), "I hope you took the baccarat to heart. We were just talking of Mrs. Bligh. I was saying that I hear she has a perfect horror of a second marriage."

The young man, in answer, gives a "HI'm!" half facetious, and wholly dubious; and both ladies laugh.

"That is what no man could ever be induced to believe about any widow!" one of them says, and then they all turn a corner and disappear.

Meanwhile the unwitting person whose name has been thus bandied about walks on, with that light step, which means in her case less youth, though she is young, than a strong, if temporary, cheerfulness, which seems to be blowing her softly along her homeward road, like a pleasant light breeze. It blows her into the door of a little clean house in Tite Street (obviously she is not rich, since she lives in Tite Street), up a narrow staircase, which yet with its white

paint and its matting dado, is not without
its claim to elegance; and into an exceedingly unpretentious, yet palm-y and daffo-
dill-y drawing-room, where her three dogs –
a woman with so many dogs must needs
be childless receive her, each after its
manner. Sally, with characteristic blunder-
ing stupidity, mistakes her for a burglar,
and rushes barking at her; Tory, too comfortable to stir out of her fireside basket,
sleepily waves a civil but not enthusiastic
tail; while poor little Twankle wreathes his
silly hairy face in joyous simpers, to express
his rapture at welcoming her back from the
perils of morning service. She answers each
one suitably, but not, as they all feel, quite
so whole - heartedly as usual, and pushing
them gently aside, walks over to the fireplace, and looks at herself in the neo-Adams
glass over the chimney-piece. As she does
so, she smiles. There are happy women
who possess faces at whose reflection one
would think they must needs always smile.
But Mrs. Bligh is not one of these; a fact

of which no one is better aware than she.
And yet presently, as she looks, her smile
grows into a laugh, and she says out loud,
as people who live alone gain a habit of
doing, " I am looking so nice, almost handsome.   Like Miss Squeers."

The dogs are so surprised at her lonely
mirth, that she laughs again ; and, in the
excess of her good spirits, catches up Tory
in her arms, and makes her also look at herself in the mirror.   But Tory has no personal
vanity, and turns away her fawn-coloured
head, bored, and yawning.   With a kiss
Mrs. Bligh sets down the pretty Sybarite,
who presently forming with the other two a
little dismal row, sends reproachful yaps
through the uprights of the balcony down
after her mistress's figure, as with a step
even cheerfuller than that which had brought
it home from church, it lessens along the
sunshiny street.   Mrs. Bligh's entertainer
lives in May Fair ; so she has plenty of
time to get up an appetite during her long
walk, by her Chelsea's squalid King's Road,

and by dull Eaton Square, up correct
Grosvenor Place, and through the Park,
where the crocuses, strewn so prettily broadcast, are beginning to push their March fires
between the grass blades. Her calculations
of her own speed must be a little out, as
she finds her hostess alone in her drawing-
room.

" How springy you look !" her friend says,
with a glance at the " mimosa bush," after
all a very modest little shrub, in her bonnet ;
" and what a colour you have got !"

" Is that a euphemistic way of telling me
my nose is red ?" replies the guest, laughing ;
yet gladdened by the flattering tone, as only
a bright-witted plain woman, whose mind
gets a great many more compliments than
her body, can be.

" Oh no, it is not at all red ; at least,
nothing to speak of," rejoins the lady of the
house absently ; being, indeed, much more
occupied by the thoughts of her approaching
luncheon party, than by care for the state of
her friend's complexion. " I am so glad you

are here so early, as I shall have time to tell you who is coming; they are all men—you will not mind that?—but I am afraid I have not got any special friend of yours."

" My men-friends might be counted upon the fingers of one hand, with a good many fingers to spare," replies Mrs. Bligh gravely. " So that is not very surprising."

" Well, there is Mr. Stanley, who is our First Secretary of Legation at Petersburg. I believe he has some awful stories about the famine in Russia."

" I hope he will not tell them at luncheon!"

" Then there is Mr. Blank, the Theosophist. He wants to become a Mahatma ; so he has lived upon slops for fifteen years."

" Will that make him a Mahatma?"

" Oh, he thinks it will help him to get up to a higher level, or some such rubbish!"

" Yes ?"

" Well, then there is the coming impressionist painter, Mr. Stannay ; you remember that portrait by him of Mrs. Glanville

Thomas in the New Gallery last year. He painted her in a strong north light, as he always does, and made such an object of her that she wanted her husband to prosecute him for libel."

" Yes ?"

" Then there is the author of that Ibsenish play, which was acted only once, because the Lord Chamberlain stopped it after the first performance—so provoking, just as I. had taken tickets. It is in the house, but I have never had time to look at it."

" What have I done to be included in so illustrious a band?" asked the visitor, half ironically, and yet half seriously too ; " but I suppose in the most *recherché* feast there must be bread and potatoes. I am your bread and potatoes."

" I may have Wyndham," pursues the hostess, still too preoccupied to pay much heed to her companion's interpolations ; " he asked me to let him leave it open ; he is perfectly worn out. They have been re-hearsing their new piece till three every morning; fancy that! but he said he would come if he possibly could."

"At every fresh celebrity you mention, I feel more and more inclined to crawl among the legs of the piano," says Mrs. Bligh, still with that mixture of irony and serious meaning; "how will you account for me? You will be as put to in explaining me as Mrs. Blanco White was the other day in the case of the solitary obscurity who had crept into one of her 'lion' parties, and whom she had to introduce as 'Mr. Smith, who—who— whose uncle was so fearfully mangled in the Tay Bridge disaster.'"

"Then there is Robert Coke, the sculptor; of course you know who I mean."

Mrs. Bligh has been all along expecting this name; so she hopes that she shows no particular emotion now that it has been pronounced.

"Sir Robert he is now," pursues the hostess, "only I always forget to call him so. You know he was K.C.B.'d the other day."

"Not K.C.B.'d," corrects Mrs. Bligh

quickly, the next instant regretting that she has done so. "The Queen made him a baronet."

"A baronet—yes, to be sure, so she did. I suppose you saw it in the papers?"

It is a careless question which does not trouble itself about an answer, and the woman to whom it is addressed would much rather not give one, and yet with a diseased honesty she thinks it necessary to reply.

"No, I did not; he told me of it himself."

"You know him?" cries the other, with an air of extreme surprise tinged with regret; "if I had known that I would have put you near him."

Mrs. Bligh is conscious of a dry inward amusement, coupled with the undoubted disappointment which she receives from the implication that her place at luncheon is not to be in the great man's neighbourhood. It is obvious that she is held to be far too obscure and uninteresting to be set within the radius of the biggest star in Lady St. George's firmament.

"I am afraid it is too late to change it now; it would entail the alteration of my whole table, and you can talk to him after luncheon."

"I have not the slightest reason for supposing that he will wish to talk to me," says Mrs. Bligh with precipitate brusqueness, and with an absurd superstitious feeling that even to imply a desire on the part of the person alluded to to converse with her will be the surest way of preventing his "changing the weather" with her.

"And so you know him?" The curiosity of the question coloured, as its object feels with a yet drier sense of amusement than before, by a distinct increase of respect. "Why, you always tell me that you do not know anybody!"

"I do not; knowing him was only an accident!"

"A very pleasant accident! I wish such accidents happened to me! Is not he delightful?"

Even Mrs. Bligh's distorted sense of

probity does not insist on her answering this question, and Lady St. George continues :

"I wonder how you came across him ? Was it at any common acquaintance of ours— at the house of anyone I know ?"

Mrs. Bligh is looking straight before her, and her voice is trenchant and dry.

"I should not think so. I met him last Christmas at the house of a relation of mine, of whose wife he was doing a bust."

"H'm! I am afraid his women are not as a rule quite as good as his men and his animals."

Mrs. Bligh reddens as if the disparagement had been of herself.

"They were all delighted with it," she says shortly and with warmth; the next second repenting of the officious ardour of her defence, the more so when she sees the vague surprise at such hot partisanship written in Lady St. George's eyes, and hears her next sincerely regretful words.

"I wish I had known earlier that you were such great friends."

" But we are not !" cries the other, in a disclaimer quite as eager as her late champion-ship. " You must not run away with such an idea ; we get on very well when we meet, but——"

Her cheeks are flushed ; her voice, never quite of Cordelia's quality, is raised in her excitement ; and her back being turned towards the door, she does not perceive that the object of discussion, who unlike all artists and most celebrities has the small but gracious virtue of punctuality, is entering the room. The sculptor has perfectly heard her resonant denial of intimacy with somebody, has instantly and justly concluded that that somebody is himself; and being a humane person, lingers over his salutation to the lady of the house, before, in answer to the latter's smiling " Here is a friend of yours !" he turns to greet her. Her mode of showing her confusion is to receive him with glacial frigidity, and as the perfect courtesy of his manner is uncoloured by any tinge of *empresse-ment*, Lady St. George feels not unnaturally that her friend has misled her. "Why did she give me to understand that they were intimate?' is her inward reflection; "they are evidently nothing of the kind." She is confirmed in this opinion by the prompt and comfortable way in which the artist drops into the corner of the sofa beside herself and remains there, while the guests arrive, and interpose their frock-coated figures between him and the lady, whom he shows no slightest symptom of a desire to approach. " He does not know that I am not to be near him at luncheon!" is the poor woman's thought. "Oh, if someone would tell him!" The aspiration in its naïf unlikeliness is worthier of a mind of seventeen than one of twenty-nine, and she realizes how far it is from being fulfilled, when, on the move to the dining-room, she finds that her allotted place is between the author of the "suppressed" drama and a young unknown, whose insignificance is sufficiently proved by the fact that he has not been thought worth including in the hostess's descriptive catalogue. For the

first moment or two her irrational disappointment - for had not she known it all along ?—
is so great that she can't lift her eyes from
her plate. Was it for this that she had but
half listened this morning to the pungent
eloquence of that great preacher? that she
had planted in her bonnet that unfitting flag
of festival, that garish, futile mimosa sprig ?
After awhile she lifts her look, and snatches
a further glance at the other end of the table
to see whether her mortification is in any
degree shared by the object of it. But a
distinguished man of fifty, renowned for the
goodness of his manners, cannot wear his
heart on his sleeve, whatever an unimportant
widow of twenty-nine may do. On his face
even she cannot find the faintest indication
of disappointment, nor if she could look into
his heart would she find much. His thoughts,
if translated into words, would probably run
thus : " Poor dear woman, I should like to
have had her next me ; but she would not
have allowed me to speak to anyone else ;
she would not have eaten a mouthful of

luncheon, or let me eat any; on the whole, it is quite as well as it is." Seeing him so philosophic, she would fain be philosophic too, and tries to throw as much life and sprightliness as a very crestfallen spirit and an unfortunately truthful nature will allow into her opening remarks to her neighbour the playwright. But whether it be that the Lord Chamberlain lies heavy on his soul, or that he does not think her worth talking to (she herself attributes it to the latter cause), he responds to her one observation so curtly that she resentfully determines not to hazard another. She must either apply herself to her fellow-obscurity on the left-hand side or address herself to listening. The diplomatist, it seems, is an old acquaintance of the sculptor's (although she flatters herself with the latter's intimacy, how little she knows of his life really!), and now, though happily reticent about the Russian famine, is telling the artist a good story. It is apparently about a celebrated actress. " You know how magnificent her proportions are now," laugh-

ing ; " well, I assure you, ten years ago she
was acting at the Gymnase in a part where
she had to fall down in a fit or a faint, or
something ; she was then such a skeleton
that a Frenchman describing it to me afterwards said, " C'était une véritable——" But
what the Frenchman said Mrs. Bligh is not
destined to hear ; for at this stage a hesitating voice at her left elbow, hesitating,
but yet loud enough effectually to drown
the point of the story, strikes in with a timid
remark :

" I think that we have an acquaintance
in common. I think that you know Miss
Smith ?"

" I know twelve compound and twenty-five
single Miss Smiths," answers she brusquely ;
but she might as well have been civiller and
more leisurely, for by the time that she can
restore her attention to what is passing at the
other end of the table both the tale and the
topic have passed by, and given place to
another. It is her own friend who is the
spokesman now, and how respectfully every-

one is listening to him! This is sure to be something really worth hearing.

"He, the Bishop, was dining one day at a house, when the footman upset a whole plate of soup down his back, right between his neck and his collar; he only looked round the table and said very mildly, 'Would some——'"

But the prelate's *bon mot* is destined to be as much lost upon Mrs. Bligh as the Parisian's, for again the irritating voice beside her interposes:

"Do not you think that it is quite a misfortune to have such a common name as Smith?"

"I know far worse misfortunes," replies the widow piquantly, turning first a homicidal look, and then a determined shoulder, upon her tormentor.

  ✳ ✳ ✳ ✳ ✳

"Who is the poor wretch whom you have been tossing and goring?" asks a caressing, good-humoured voice in her ear, as she leaves the dining-room. "I am glad it is not me this time!" and after all her anticipations, this is the sum of her conversation with her friend.

CHAPTER II.

IF, like Richard II.'s queen, Mrs. Bligh had set forth :

"Adorned hither, like sweet May,"

she is certainly, as was that poor lady,

"Sent back like Hallowmas, or shortest day."

She has scarcely energy enough to turn the latchkey in her own door, or to climb the stairs, which all the dogs—even lazy Tory— come trundling noisily down to meet her. They can hardly believe their ears when she crossly bids them get out of her way. But there is a far severer disappointment in store for them than that caused by any want of amenity in her manner, when they by-and-by discover that their earthly providence is not going to take them for their usual Sunday walk. They watch her nervously as she irritably pulls up the blinds, rattles the poker among the sleeping coals, and finally throwing off her cloak, flings herself into an armchair. One slight spark of hope lingers in their minds, from the fact of her not having taken off her bonnet, but by-and-by even this dies out. It is difficult for a kindhearted person to resist the urgent entreaty of six humbly insistent eyes, and though in the case of Mrs. Bligh's dogs the number is reduced to five— since Sall was relieved of one in early life by a cat—her will generally melts like wax before the fire of that mutely eloquent joint stare. To-day she is obdurate. It is not that she is At Home on Sundays, being rather new to London, with few acquaintances and less belief in any ardent desire on the part of those few to see her.

The one person whom she had credited with a taste for her conversation has to-day with unmistakable plainness shown her her error. That she should ever have fallen into

so gross a one makes her face blaze now into
a flame, not kindled by the sulky fire, before
which she lies in her armchair—blaze so that
even the dogs' eyes trouble her and she puts
up both hands to hide them out, while from
between her fingers ejaculations such as
" Fool!" " Idiot!" " Fatuous folly!" shoot
out, uttered aloud into the silent and empty
room. Looked back upon now, the founda-
tions on which she had built her towering
superstructure of hopes of his notice and
belief in his interest are seen to be flimsy
in the extreme. What are they, these foun-
dations, when examined with coolness and
reason? Three months ago she had accidentally met him at an inexpressibly dull
Dorsetshire manor-house, whither his work
had brought him, and where a snow-fall had
detained him, bitterly against his will.
Through five dreary days of frozen captivity
she—her indifferent jokes, her slight smatter-
ing knowledge of the books he loved, her
stupidly undisguised admiration for himself—
had been the refuge of his *ennui;* a fact he

has recognised and shown his generous gratitude for since, by spending upon her two or
three of his rare half-hours of leisure and
liberty.   Until to-day she has never met him
in any company except her own, or that of
her bucolic cousins, has never seen him in
the " Milieu " in which he habitually lives.
Amid the polyglot company at luncheon there
had been no ladies for him to wound her
feelings by showing any preference for over
her, none except the hostess, who had been
far too much occupied in making her party
go off to have leisure or inclination for private dalliance with any one member of it,
even the leading lion.   Yet, as Mrs. Bligh's
memory recalls the half-words so immediately
understood, the allusions so instantly grasped
by her friend which in most cases had been
Greek to her she has an uncomfortable sen-
sation of having been out of it, of being the
hungry little street-boy staring in through the
window at the Christmas roast goose into
which he will never thrust his knife.   Out of
it !   Out of his life !   Out of his interests !

Out of all but his charity ! As he would give an old woman in a workhouse half a pound of tea, or a screw of tobacco, so he has thrown her ten civil words or a kind look, and she has mistaken these paltry alms for the magnificent gift of his equal friendship. This is no doubt reserved for the feminine part of that society with the masculine half of which she has to-day seen him on such terms of gay cordiality. He has always told her that he greatly prefers women to men. If, then, such is the heartiness and warmth of his manner to the husbands and fathers, what must it be to the wives and daughters ? She knows that he is always at home on Sundays, receiving his friends in his studio, on a general invitation, which he has extended to her, but of which she has hitherto been too shy to avail herself.

Lying dismally in her rumpled armchair, she pictures him doing the honours of his beloved atelier, surrounded by beautiful women who are going to sit to him, by witty women with whom he is exchanging flashing

repartees, by sympathetic women, to whom
he is explaining his ideas before they are
translated into stone.   Mrs. Bligh is one of
the many Englishwomen who gratuitously
embitter their lives by cold Sunday supper
instead of dinner, and by allowing her
servants a right of almost universal exodus,
ending in the crowning gaiety, so dear to
every servant's heart, of evening church.
The result to herself is a crop of small discomforts, in unremoved tea-table, late and
ill-lit lamps, and oddly announced visitors,
whose names suffer strange metamorphoses
in the mouth of an unaccustomed underling.
To this latter inconvenience she has not been
exposed to day, since she has had no callers,
and now it is too late to expect any, as the
clock's finger points to a quarter to seven.
The idea strikes her rather bitterly that
London out of all its five millions has not
spared one friendly human face and voice to
her.   Shall she go to evening church like the
servants ?   No, she will not offer her bore-
dom to God.   But she will, at all events, put

an end to this contemptible and idle puling over the inevitable, and will ring for the tarrying lights, to help her by occupation to rout her demon of discontent and sloth. She rises and pulls the bell, thinking, as it peals through the house, how like it is in sound to the hall-door one, which has hung so idle through the long afternoon. She does not again sit down, but stands with foot on fender, and hot forehead leant against the white wood of the chimneypiece, a position she still keeps when the door opens in answer, as she supposes, to her ring.

"Bring the lamps!" she says, with her head still lying sideways on the mantelshelf, but her languid order is drowned in a universal uprising rush and clamour of the dogs. Why should they bark so loudly at their own familiar scullion? Their mistress raises her head to put this question to them, and finds herself facing one who is strangely dressed for a kitchen-maid in a gray frock-coat and a head to match—a head that, though grizzly, is thick clad and curly.

" It's you, is it ?" she says in an odd jerky voice, and though her visitor knows her and her voice rather well, he has a moment of misgiving that he is not welcome.

" Send me away if I am too late," he says apologetically. " I am late. I see you have got rid of all your other friends."

" They were such a crowd that they had a difficulty in squeezing through the door," replies she, laughing dryly, adding, with an ungraciousness oddly out of harmony with her real feelings. " I thought that you were always at home on Sundays ?"

" Do not speak in that ferocious voice," replies the sculptor, looking round for a safe place on which to deposit his hat and stick out of reach of the dogs, and, having found it, subsiding on to a *pouf* at his hostess's feet. " Are you going to dance on me as you did on that unhappy innocent at luncheon ?"

Her breath comes a little fast with the pleasure of seeing these indications of a proposed stay on the part of her visitor, but her answer does not display much softness.

" If I danced it was the Dance of Death ! Did you ever see anything so ill-managed ? Was not I wretchedly placed ? I could not help thinking of a tale of a friend of mine who was sent into dinner with a terrific bore, and in the middle of the feast burst out crying from sheer *ennui*. I could have followed her example without any difficulty."

He looks up at her—her chair is on a much higher level than his low seat - startled, perhaps a little disturbed at the unnecessary vehemence of her expressions of annoyance, and for the moment has no rejoinder ready.

" Well, at all events, somebody was pleased," continues Mrs. Bligh; " you were in your element ; you, at least, enjoyed yourself."

" I !" repeats he, with an air of extreme surprise ; " my dear lady, you must be joking. I went because our hostess has never ceased asking me to luncheon since last Christmas twelvemonth ; and because "— with a timely, if not very sincere afterthought

" because I knew that I was to have the pleasure of meeting you there."

She is aware that the last clause of this sentence is not strictly true, but it gives her such pleasure to even half believe it that she lets it pass undisputed.

" And you know," he adds with a smile, whose sweetness takes away any of the implied rebuke that his words might seem to convey, " you know that, pleasant as it would undoubtedly be, one cannot always wear one's heart outside without inconvenience."

" I know one cannot," she answers ; " though it is where for nine-and-twenty ill-spent years I have carried mine !" Then, hurrying shyly away from the subject of that organ which between man and woman can seldom be dispassionately discussed, " If you were not enjoying yourself at luncheon, you were at least the cause of enjoyment in others. What good stories you and your friend were telling ! I am sure they were good, though that little miscreant beside me prevented my ever reaching their point. What do you think he kept asking me, while I was straining my ears to catch your *bons mots*— whether I knew Miss Smith ? I answered that I knew two hundred and fifty Miss Smiths, and begged him to hold his tongue."

"I should not think he needed much begging after that," says Coke with a smile, and a half-thought of what an impossible woman to make love to this odd, prickly little friend of his would be.

"Did I know Miss Smith ?" repeats she, with an ire that is half put on, because she feels that it is amusing him, and yet is half sincere too.

"I do not know whether you did, but I know a Miss Smith," rejoins Coke, still lazily amused at her vehemence ; "that is to say, I know one more Miss Smith than I did yesterday—not a hard, plain Smith, but some pretty little compound, though I cannot remember what it was. She was brought to my studio by an old Gorgon, to whom I have to be civil because she is ordering a big fountain with river gods and a little Nereid—I must show you the clay sketch, dear friend—

for her place in Bedfordshire ; and this little
wild rose Smith came with her, and she
knows you, and loves you, and we made
great friends over you !"

" Was it Pamela Capel-Smith ?" asks Mrs.
Bligh, sitting upright in her chair, with her
eyes alight with interest.

He shakes his head smiling.

" We did not get to Christian names,
though at the rate we were going we might
have done in another quarter of an hour, if
that old Medusa had not carried her off."

" If it was Pamela," says the widow with
emphasis, " she is a darling."

" Then it was Pamela," returns he, laughing, " for she was a darling ; you, at least,
ought to say so, for she raved about you."

A colour that is by no means wholly born
of pleasure runs over Mrs. Bligh's face.

" I wish she would not ; it is so silly of
her. I hope you stopped her."

" Why should I ? On the contrary, *j'abon-
dais dans le même sens ;* but, seriously, she
spoke of you with enthusiastic admiration."

" I cannot think what possesses her," says the object of this commendation, in a tone of such unaffected wonder and disgust that her companion laughs outright. " I could understand her liking me," continues she; "there are things in me that might breed a moderate liking; but what is there in me, I ask you, which could command enthusiastic admiration ?"

As she speaks she fixes on her hearer her eager and intelligent eyes; and since his own feeling for her, though sincere, is quite untinged with ecstasy, and she is too much in earnest to be put off with a compliment, he is for a moment at a loss for a reply. Then—

" She told me," he says, with a half-hesitating glance at an invalid chair standing in evident disuse against the wall of the back drawing-room, " of what a hard life you had had, and with what wonderful pluck you had borne it." Her eye follows the direction of his glance, and her lower lip twitches. " Why have you never talked to me about your

past ?" he inquires in a tone of very nearly
tender reproach ; "why did you leave me to
learn from a little stranger chit what a heroine
you have been !"

"But I have not !" cries she, her trenchant
denial leaping out with the violence as of one
rebutting the accusation of a crime. " If she
told you so, she grossly misrepresented.
Come now, what has she told you ?"

The person thus challenged again hesitates
for an instant. It may be roughly averred
that none of us speak of our friends behind
their backs precisely as we should to their
faces ; and in the present instance Coke is
aware of the need of adapting and Bowd-
lerising the statements of his young informant
about the departed Bligh, so as to render
them palatable to his widow.

" She told me," he says slowly, and feeling
his way, "about your marriage ; that your
husband was paralyzed almost from the beginning of it, and that you nursed him for
eight years devotedly and without a murmur !"

" Without a murmur!" repeats she, and her voice, although this time almost inaudibly low, expresses a disclaimer of the virtues attributed to her, even more emphatic than her former vociferous one. " Why, I did nothing but murmur! Looking back upon it now, it seems to me as if I had never done anything else !"

" She told me how wonderfully patient you had been under the——"

He stops, uncertain how best to paraphrase the communication that had been made to him : " Though he was paralyzed, he had the temper of a devil, and used to throw things at her head."

" I never was patient, it is not in me to be ; I was dreadfully sorry for him ; yes, that I was " (her voice shaking a little), " though I do not know whether he believed even that, and I had a bad time of it. I had not been married six weeks when it began—creeping paralysis ; and from that on to the end——" She pauses expressively. " Yes, I had a bad time ; but, after all, what was it in comparison of *his!* a soul as much alive as yours or mine, in a half-dead body?" Again she pauses. " And yet I often spoke crossly to him, often. He was naturally irritable ; who would not have been?" A vision of three-legged stools hurtling through the air passes before the hearer's mental eye. "And of course I ought to have understood that it was only disease, and put up with it, but I did not. Often, often, I answered him as impatiently as——"

" As your neighbour at luncheon to-day ?" half playfully. But she is in downright desperate earnest.

" As badly as that—worse ! It seems incredible now ; but I did. I kept that chair," again glancing towards the back room, " to remind me of it!" Her voice has grown harsh, an effect which emotion always produces upon it, as she winds up with : " So you'll know for the future how much to believe of the pretty things that admiring girls tell you about me !"

There is a silence, infringed only by a

foolish bark from Tory, as she catches the sound of a dog's step in the street outside, being never able to realize that that thoroughfare is not her private property.

CHAPTER III.

COKE has not the least notion how to respond
to that embarrassing remark about the *chaise
longue*, whose ugly presence, cramming up
his friend's little back room, his artistic eye
has several times revolted against, though
some instinct has happily preserved him from
telling her so. She herself comes to his
rescue.

"Well," she cries brusquely, "we have
had quite enough of me for one while; let us
have a little of you for a change. How is
'Rayon d'Or' getting on?" (naming a famous
Derby winner). "Is he to be in bronze or
marble?"

"The duke cannot make up his mind,"

replies Coke, hoping that the relief in his voice at the changed turn the conversation has taken is not as evident to her as it is to himself.

"And is he to stand on two legs or four? I mean" (laughing) "not the duke, but the horse!"

"I can't make up my mind; you must" (caressingly) "come and make it up for me."

"You are so apt to ask for advice about your work, and I am so competent to give it," answers she dryly; but she colours faintly with pleasure all the same.

They are both standing now—he preparing to go, and she to bid him good-bye—each with a foot on the fender, and an elbow on the chimneypiece; they face each other comfortably in the firelight.

"When will you come? Since I knew you, you have been to the studio only——" He stops, for the life of him he can't recall the exact number of her visits. But her memory is more retentive:

"Only twice; and for the present it will

have to remain only twice, since I am going out of London."

"You?"

"Yes, I! *Moi qui vous parle!* all the rest of the nobility and gentry" (smiling) "are turning out for Easter; why should not I, too?'

"You are always gadding, madam; and where are you going—to Dorsetshire?" with a rather lowered voice, and a not very sincere sigh, paid to the memory of his sojourn in that dreary county.

"No, not to Dorsetshire," her voice lagging with unconscious tenderness over the dear name. "Geography is not a very strong point with me, nor with you, either; but I fancy it is a good deal in the other direction that I am going; it is to the Isle of Anglesey!"

"Are you going to look for Lycidas ' on the shaggy top of Mona high?' "

"That was not my leading motive" (again smiling); "but I dare say mine will turn out nearly as much of a fool's errand as that would be. I am going to visit a friend of my childhood, whom I have not seen since—since——"

"Since you were short-coated?" with hurried jocosity, to avert an apprehended drifting back into the painful memories of her married life. That the effort is successful is apparent by her next remark, thoughtfully uttered :

"When last she saw me my hair was down to my knees and my petticoats up to them ; how am I to prove to her that I am I?"

"It cuts both ways. How is she to prove to you that she is she?"

"She cannot be as much altered as I am ; in the first place, when we parted, her skirts were already long, and her hair short. She is three years older than I. We were school friends. I was a wretched ugly little girl, and she was a fine buxom big one. She always promised me that I should stay with her when she was married! Neither of us ever faced so unlikely a possibility as my marrying."

"She has taken some time in fulfilling her promise."

"That was not her fault. I never could go anywhere, pay any visits during—while——"

"Yes, yes," hastily ; "I understand, and—she has a husband living ?"

"Yes, an exceptionally attractive one, so she tells me ; and she has a child and two grown-up step-children, and oxen and sheep and camels and asses, and a place in Anglesey on the Menai Straits."

"No wonder that you cannot resist such a list of attractions. Anglesey !" wrinkling his forehead in the effort to recapture an illusive recollection. "Where have I been hearing of Anglesey lately ? Oh, I know ! only yesterday I got a letter, dated from some crackjaw Welsh Plas there ; it was from a Sir Somebody Something—his name escapes me—ordering a monument for his late mother. He writes to me" (looking amused) "rather as if I were a working stonemason ! Perhaps" (with a sudden inspiration) "he may turn out to be your friend's husband, the exceptionally attractive husband of whom "— moving his gray coat-sleeve somewhat nearer her black one on the mantelshelf—" I am already a little jealous."

"No, he is not a Sir. He is only a plain Mr."

"Well, you must find out all about him for me—all about him and his 'late mother.' He wishes her to be recumbent like Lady ——, only without the baby."

"Yes?"

"And if you find that he is a great Crœsus—I expect he has slate quarries—and that Anglesey is very paradisaical, it might be worth my while to run down for a day or two. No, no!"—marking, and half startled by the illumination of her whole face at the suggestion. "I am only joking! Delightful as it would be, I could not possibly spare the time."

"Of course not—of course not!"

"Shall you take all the dogs?" stooping to pull Sall's ear, as with her one eye rolling

she stands up fat and tall, clawing his knee
to attract his attention, though when she has
gained it she has evidently nothing particular
to say to him. "I should like to do a little
group of you, with your dogs, in terra-cotta.
I could make a pretty thing of it!"

"You are a very clever man, but you are
not quite clever enough for that," replies she,
with one of her habitual and injudicious fleers
at her own appearance; since there is no such
undoubted fact than that we are all valued at
our own appraisement.

"And when do you go?"

"On Wednesday."

"And I shall not see you again?" in a
regretful tone, and with a still further en-
croachment on her half of the chimney-piece
by the gray elbow.

"I suppose not," wistfully—so wistfully
that he breaks out into a hurried explanation.

"It is most unlucky; but these two next
days are specially busy ones with me. To-
morrow H.R.H. comes at five. Royalties
are often late, and of course I do not know

how long he will stay; and on Tuesday
I have to go down into the country to
get some more sketches of Rayon d'Or,
and——"

"Of course, I had not the least expectation
of seeing you again," interrupts she, her
harsh touch reappearing in her voice with
the fear of having seemed exacting, adding
stiffly, "it was very good of you to come this
evening."

"It was very good of you to let me in.
Your little maid—the Sunday *locum tenens*,
is not she?—did not much like my looks.
She made such a funny face, like a gargoyle;
she is rather like one of those heads on the
spouts at Nuremberg. I must ask her to sit
to me; do you give your consent?"

"You have my full permission!" replies
she; and he goes away laughing, while she
remains behind, staring into the neglected
fire with a rather sardonic smile, and a re-
flective wonder as to which work of art will
give her distinguished friend the greatest
pleasure in the execution: the terra-cotta

group of herself and her dogs, or the gargoyle
head of the kitchen-maid? The latter is
fated to have another shock before the evening
is done. Mrs. Bligh is lingering over her
cold chicken and claret, less from any lively
enjoyment of them than from a reluctance to
return to her now doubly-empty drawing-
room, when the hall-door bell once again
peals. The idea instantly flashes across the
widow's mind that it is a commissionaire
bearing a note from her late visitor. After
all, he has found an unoccupied half-hour
somewhere lurking in the compass of the
next two days. "Where there is a will there
is a way," and evidently in this case there is
a will, is her exulting reflection. But this
towering frame of mind lasts only during the
short space that it takes a quick young foot
to cross the little hall, an impatient young
hand to open the door, and a fur-wrapped
young figure to come skipping in.

"Pamela!"

"Yes, Anne, Pamela! Am I too late?"
her face falling at the not very decided wel-

come of the word and tone. " Send me
away if I am !"

It strikes Mrs. Bligh with a slight and
fanciful annoyance, which she would be
puzzled to explain, that both her guests have
employed exactly the same words with which
to conjure her displeasure at their unexpected
appearance.

" I left them all at dinner—my people, I
mean ; they think I have gone to bed. I had
to come and tell you of something so exciting
that has happened. Who do you think I
have met ? Whose acquaintance do you
suppose I have made to-day ? Ah !" something in her listener's face revealing that her
tidings come too late—" you have heard
already ? He has told you ? He has been
here since ? How delightful !"

" Delightful for whom ?" playfully, and yet
not very playfully, either ; " for me or for
him ?"

" Oh, for him most ; of course, much the
most for him," her nut-brown eyes shining
with affectionate enthusiasm ; " but nice for

you, too " (laughing), " to have such a celebrity basking on your hearthrug. I had such a happy talk with him about you. You should have seen how cleverly he put off that tiresome Lady ——, who took me to his studio, and who wanted to bore him all the time about a fountain he is designing for her. He stopped her mouth playfully, you know ; not in the least so that she could take offence, but yet quite effectually."

" She will probably, to-morrow, order her fountain elsewhere."

" I never heard anything more neatly done. I wish I could remember the exact words."

" Do not try. Nobody's good things bear carrying, except Sidney Smith's."

" We talked of nothing but you," continues the young stranger, her voice unconsciously taking a less jubilant inflection, as she feels that the great news, to carry which, hot and fresh, she had forfeited her dinner, is falling unaccountably flat. " You should have seen the change in his manner the

moment he found that I was a friend of yours.
I told him what extraordinary luck it was for
me, your having taken me up."

"I wish you would not!" exclaims the
other, impatiently pushing about the spoons
and forks on the dinner-table. Then, ashamed
of her own irritability, "Let us come upstairs. I do not want to regale you with the
fumes of my funeral-baked meats; it is fune-
real "—casting a disgusted look at her lonely
repast—"eating by one's self, is not it?"
Arrived at the drawing-room—"I am speaking quite seriously," says the widow, still
battling not very successfully with a certain
tartness of voice. "I do wish you would try
to choose a better subject for your enthusiasm.
I know that you mean it very kindly, but it
makes me look such a fool! as if I encouraged
you in your ludicrously exaggerated estimate
of my merits."

The pretty creature thus lectured looks
rather crestfallen.

"I do not rave about you to everybody—
not to *le premier venu*," she says, her fresh

red under-lip quivering a little. " I choose people who I know will be in sympathy with me. He was quite in sympathy, quite as enthusiastic as I! He was so interested in things I told him about you—about your past life." Anne's mouth breaks into a vexed yet half-humorous smile.

"My dear, I spent half an hour by Shrewsbury clock in contradicting all your statements. Can't you see the brutality of giving a poor woman a character that she cannot possibly live up to—that she must be found out in, even by 'a celebrity basking on her hearthrug'?"

" But the celebrity is quite as foolish about you as I am."

Anne shakes her head almost angrily.

" Did you ever hear of a monosyllable called ' Fudge'?"

"Yes, I have; but it has no applicability here; however, I will not tease you, since you do not like it. Time"—confidently—"will show which of us is right, and meanwhile I have another bit of good news to tell you."

"Another?" Mrs. Bligh's eyebrows had moved up slightly. The tidings as yet brought seem to her scarcely to merit the title of an Evangel.

"Yes; I am to be allowed after all to go to Anglesey to visit the Mulhollands at the same time as you. I am even to go on Wednesday. We may travel together. I shall have you"—smiling radiantly—"all to myself from Euston to Beaumaris."

"I travel third-class."

"I do not mind. I have no doubt that it will amuse me very much."

"Your experience will be different from mine, then. Travelling third-class often disgusts me, often makes me angry, but it never amuses me. However, if anything can cure you of your amiable craze, travelling with me will. A railway journey with me means an unbroken hand-to-hand tussle with my fellow-travellers over the window!"

"I will tussle too."

They both laugh, and then Pamela, in a tone of stifled excitement :

"I am dying to know what you will think of them all."

"I am growing rather nervous on that head myself, too. Come, describe them all over again to me. Mrs. Mulholland first, the friend of my frilled trousers days."

"Oh, she is a dear splunchy old thing!"

"That is a comfort, at all events"—dryly —"but would you mind explaining what 'splunchy' means?"

"Oh, do not you know what 'splunchy' means? I think it is such an expressive word, there is nothing quite synonymous: 'splunchy' means—well—'splunchy'!"

"That is about as lucid a definition as Bardolph's of 'accommodated.'"

"Well, she is a dear, soft, pillowy kind of old thing."

"Old thing! Are you aware what a dagger you are planting in my breast? She is exactly three years older than I."

"Impossible!"—with growing indignation —"she might be your mother! I think she tries to make herself look as old as she can to match him."

" And the stepdaughter ?"

" Lucile ? Oh, she is, as she herself would express it, 'a ripper.' She is given over to horses, and dogs, and donkeys."

" And my friend's own child ?"

" Little Sue ? Oh, she is a ripper, too."

" They are all rippers, in fact ; and the father, Mr. Mulholland, is the greatest ripper of all, no doubt ?"

The answer to this last query does not come so trippingly as to the former ones.

" I do not think I should quite describe Mr. Mulholland as a ripper."

" He is very gifted, isn't he ? witty, accomplished, distinguished-looking ?"

The girl hesitates even more perceptibly than before.

" Ye-es, I dare say. I suppose so."

" His wife has certainly always implied it."

" Oh, she worships him !"

" And his children, do they worship him, too ?"

"Yes"—with an accent of involuntary wonder and dissent — "they think him splendid."

Mrs. Bligh smiles.

"It is very obvious that you do not agree with them."

"I! oh no!"—vehemently—"I ha——' she pulls herself up short. "It is not of the least consequence what I think. I am a wretched judge of character. I will not tell you anything more about any of them. It will be much more amusing for you to find everything out for yourself."

CHAPTER IV.

IT is obvious that H.R.H.'s visit to Sir Robert Coke's studio must have been prolonged to quite the expected length on Thursday afternoon, and that Rayon d'Or must have swallowed up all Tuesday, for on neither of those days, though she foolishly stays within doors for the best part of most of them, does Mrs. Bligh receive any suggestion of a rendezvous from her sculptor friend. And on Wednesday she goes. Her departure is in a windy pour of cold rain, and as she watches the dirty moisture rolling down the sacking-covered back of the stone-deaf old driver of the four-wheeler which conveys her to Euston, she asks herself, with too-late in-

dignation, what is taking her on such a fool's
errand ? She repeats the question internally
as she stands at the door of a rapidly-filling
third-class carriage, trying alternately, and
with equal ill-success, to glare away from her
compartment the third-class babies who too
obviously have their eye upon it, and to
dissuade her young admirer from sharing her
own too certain discomforts. But Pamela,
radiant with the double brilliance born of
happy expectation, and of a really good complexion in wet weather, keeps her ground
stoutly beside the object of her cult, asseve-
rating with every appearance of sincerity that
it will be very amusing, and that she shall
enjoy it of all things. Finding the uselessness
of her remonstrances, the widow desists, and
remains standing on the platform, glancing
with silent indifference at its occupants, until
she catches sight of a figure which causes
her to give utterance to an exclamation of
dismay.

"Oh, good heavens, there is that dreadful
bore ! Let us get in quick. I do not sup-

pose that he would recognise me again, but he might."

"What dreadful bore?" following the direction of her friend's eyes, and scanning the passers-by with a puzzled air.

"I met him at luncheon at Lady St. George's on Sunday. Oh, he is such a bore! I should die if he got into the carriage with us."

"I do not quite see who you mean," still vaguely gazing about.

"He has stopped at the book-stall to buy a paper. There! do not you see? that man in the brown overcoat, with a plaid over his arm."

"That man," repeats Pamela, having at length succeeded in discriminating the object of Anne's animadversions from the other hurrying or sauntering travellers, while her face expresses a surprise that is rather acute than pleasant. "Why, that is young Mulholland!"

"Young Mulholland?"

"Yes, young Mulholland; your friend's

stepson. You knew, did not you, that she
had a stepson as well as a stepdaughter?"

"How truly dreadful!" cries the other, in
a voice that sounds disproportionately aghast
for the occasion. "I did not catch his name
on Sunday; if I had, of course I should—I
mean I should not——"

She breaks off, while memory recalls to
her with officious vividness the gratuitous
incivility of her own manner to one who now
perversely turns out to be her host.

"I think," says the girl, turning only the
edge of a very rosy cheek to her companion,
"that he means—that he intends to travel
down by this train."

"Of course you were the Miss Smith
whom he tried to talk to me about," cries
Mrs. Bligh, with a very annoyed laugh, as
unpleasant little accesses of enlightenment
keep pressing in upon her mind. "It was
about you that I snubbed him so ferociously.
Oh, why does not one make a rule to be
always civil *quand même!* What frightful
retributions overtake one! Oh, here he

comes! I really can't face him," vaulting into the carriage as she speaks, over the bags and bottles already established there, diving into its farthest corner and sitting down with her nose against the pane.

She does not again look round till the train is in motion, and even then the glance she throws over the occupants of the compartment is an apprehensive one. But what it shows her is reassuring. An Anglican clergyman, five working women, a blue-jacket, a carpenter with a bag of tools, and a couple of infants. But no young gentleman in brown. Her eye meets her friend's opposite with an expression of relief in it.

"You got in in time, then. He did not see us."

"Yes, he did"—hesitating somewhat—" I think he meant to get in too, but I told him —I persuaded him not."

"Good heavens!" cries Anne, observing the want of readiness with which this explanation is given, while a new billow of remorse and dismay rushes over her. "I

believe that he is a dear friend of yours—
that it was an appointment." If the girl
colours it is almost invisibly.

"Oh, he is not bad in his way ; I like him
very well in his right place, as people say
about dogs when they do not care about
them"—laughing—" but"—with a reproachful
accent—" do you suppose—can you imagine
that I want him, or anything else, when I
have you ?"

The widow's sole answer to this declaration is a good-humoured " Pooh !" and she
leans back in her hard corner, thinking that
she is as little able to rise to her young
votary's height of devotion as was Catherine
Morland to reciprocate Isabella Thorpe's
declaration of how much dearer she —
Catherine—would be to her than her own
sisters. The journey is long, and, as to discomfort, much what might have been expected. The adult portion of the two ladies'
fellow-travellers eat obnoxious viands, and
drink nose - offending liquids almost un-
brokenly throughout its course, and the

babies go with unblushing publicity through all the unpleasant gymnastics common to third-class babies on their travels. Both Pamela and Anne have long sunk into a jaded silence by the time that the sight of the incoming tide splashing the Welsh coast, along which the London and North-Western Railway runs, revives their flagging spirits.

"We shall not be long now," says the younger encouragingly. "And they are sure to send to meet us. I hope they will send something open."

"Is it a long drive?"

"Six miles! Beaumaris is five miles from a station, and they are a mile beyond Beaumaris. It is a long way; but it keeps the trippers off, so I think on the whole they are glad."

"Yes."

"It is a lovely road: shaded by trees, and running along above the Menai Straits. Now that there are no leaves on the trees, you can see both them and the mountains opposite beautifully."

" Yes."

" They will probably send the waggonette, and most likely "—with a fresh access of hesitation —" young Mulholland will drive us himself; you will not mind that? You will not mind his being on the box ?"

Anne breaks into a vexed laugh.

" My dear child, not mind my host's son taking the liberty of sitting in his own father's carriage ! What can you think I am made of ? Like Cleopatra, ' Tho' I am mad, I will not bite him !' "

" Oh no ; it is only that you said you thought him such a dreadful bore !"

" For pity's sake "—impatiently—" do not quote me against myself, as Madame de Sevigné said about her tiresome friend : ' Dieu me fait la grâce de ne pas l'écouter ;' so *Dieu me fait la grâce* never to remember my own speeches ! In mercy, try to imitate me ! They are never worth remembering."

" On the contrary, your judgment is so excellent, that I feel sure you are right. I have no doubt that he is a bore. I wonder "

—thoughtfully—"that it never struck me before."

"And I am sure he is nothing of the kind," with a too late compunctious effort to repair the mischief she has done, and repenting, for not the first time in her life by many, her inability to keep her tongue between her teeth.

Third-class passengers seldom possess ladies' maids, and Mrs. Bligh is accustomed, though never wholly reconciled, to the necessity of wrestling for her own luggage. She is preparing to do so when at length deposited on the platform of the remote Welsh station to which she is bound. But her intention is forestalled by a young man in brown, who has instantly joined her companion, and who, whether goaded to the action by the latter, or inspired by the Christianity of his own spirit, now approaches herself with lifted hat, and, with a look and voice of ill-disguised terror, asks her leave to find her boxes for her.

"I do not know why you should have

that trouble," replies she abashed, while
memory thrusts upon her the tart request to
hold his tongue which had been her last
observation to him. " There are two ; both
have a large A. B. on them, and a red and
white stripe ; but I really do not know why
you should take the trouble."

He is out of hearing before she has half
finished her apologies, and only Pamela has
the benefit of them.

" His manner is very bad," says the girl
apologetically, and yet in a critical tone
which Anne guiltily feels to be no older than
her own uncomplimentary remarks upon him.
" So abrupt, as if he wanted to bite your
head off ; but I think he means to be civil."

" I am sure he does," cries Anne eagerly ;
and in a minute more he is back with them ;
and in her haste to make an *amende* for her
former lack of civility, she rushes into a well-
intended but brusque pleasantry, as to the
large coal fire he has been making on the top
of her head.

He looks perfectly blank, and she is

obliged to give a lame explanation of her
meaning, which lasts till they reach the
waggonette. The reflection of how far more
tactful it would have been to have let sleeping dogs lie, and ignored their former meeting, spoils the first quarter of a mile of her
drive. But the thud of the horses' feet as they
trot across the airy suspension bridge flung
over the sea's arm, the salt taste of the air
after the noisome closeness of the train, and,
lastly, her young *vis-à-vis* bubbling joy and
pride in doing the honours of the lovely road
which they pursue, soon restore her equanimity.

"That is Penmaen Mawr!" pointing
through the naked arch of the tree-boughs,
and across the sun-dancing water of the
Straits, "that great round-headed hill, with
the slopes of shale ; do not you remember we
passed right under it ? No, you can't see
Snowdon ; it is too far back. There is
General ——'s place that we are passing.
Mrs. Mulholland took me to call there once ;
it is so pretty inside ; the garden runs down
quite to the water. Here "—as they stop at

a gate—" we go along a private road that Sir Thomas Lascelles has made on a higher level than the public one ; he is the local swell here, and the Mulhollands' little grounds join his big ones, which he allows them to use as if they were their own."

" Sir Thomas Lascelles," repeats Anne, as her memory recalls the nameless Welsh baronet and art patron concerning whom Sir Robert Coke had desired her to make inquiries. " Does he live at Glan something, and is he—had he a mother?"

The girl looks naturally a little surprised at the idiotic shape taken by the latter half of these inquiries.

" Glan y Wern. It is a magnificent place, and I suppose he had a mother once : he has not now."

" Did she die lately ?"

" I do not know ; they are not in mourning. Why do you ask ?"

" Oh, I—I—had no particular reason— mere idle curiosity,' shirking, as usual, the necessity of mentioning her sculptor.

She is saved from the danger of having to give any more intelligible explanation of her question by young Mulholland, who now throws a remark from the box over his shoulder—not at her, though it would be easier so to do, since she is sitting on the opposite side to him, but at Pamela.

" Lucile is laid up again."

" You do not say so! I thought her sprain was better."

" So it was, and they said she might take a quiet little drive ; but her idea of a quiet little drive was to put the two donkeys tandem into that coster's cart I made her ; and in going through a gate, the new one— the leader—mischievously shut it behind him, leaving the cart and the wheeler on the other side ; so she was spilt, and she is as bad as ever now."

" Poor Lucile!"

" Is she—is your sister very fond of driving tandem?" asks Mrs. Bligh, with a second, and this time not in the least facetious, attempt at conciliation.

But the young man either thinks, or pretends
to think, that the inquiry can't be addressed to
him ; and it would have fallen with perfect
flatness to the ground had not Pamela, red
with indignation, picked it up.

" Mrs. Bligh is speaking to you, George ;
she is asking you whether Lucile is not very
fond of driving tandem ?"

The question thus repeated seemed as
worthless in its original owner's ears as do
the twice or thrice-shouted inanities which
we have all, in our day, shamefacedly bawled
into a deaf man's ear, and she makes no
further effort.   They have trotted through a
drowsy little town—saved from vulgar ex-
pansion by its distance from a railway—along
a stone-walled, white road, into a modest
drive, and are nearing a good-sized, early
Victorian house with a tower, which stands
looking at the lovely Straits.

" I am feeling quite jumpy !" says Anne,
with a nervous laugh.   " Am I tidy ?—is my
bonnet straight ?"

" Perfectly ; you are always so beautifully

neat, not a hair out of place ; nothing could
look nicer than you do !"

Though not wholly crediting these agreeable assurances, the widow is yet a little
comforted by them ; and her eye follows that
of her young friend, which is looking eagerly
out ahead, and who now breaks out into
pleased exclamations.

" Ah, I knew how it would be ! As soon
as they heard the wheels they would come
flying out ! They are at the door !"

"What, all the 'rippers'?" asks Anne,
hiding her real shyness under a rather uncertain merriment—"all except the sick
one ?"

There is no time for more, as they have
drawn up at the porticoed door, at which a
fair, fat woman, a long-leggy little girl with an
irregularly delightful face, and some servants,
are grouped ; and in another moment the fat
woman and Anne are standing looking at each
other with undisguised stupefaction, and saying severally, and with equal brilliancy :

" Here you are !" and " Yes, here we are !"

In yet another moment they are in the drawing-room, and have bethought themselves that they ought to kiss, which—such utter strangers do they appear to one another —they do with a little hesitation. The small familiarity loosens the string of their tongues.

"Is it really and truly you, Nan?" cries the hostess, still holding her guest's hand, and peering at her features with an air of friendly incredulity.

"Nan!" repeats the other, in a rather tremulous key. "How many, many years it is since anyone called me Nan! Yes, Char, I am Nan, though I sometimes doubt it myself! I believe," laughing shyly, "that you expected to see me still in frilled trousers!"

"Ah, that is more like you"—in a tone of relief—"that is just the way in which you used to say things at school. How droll you were, and how you used to make us laugh!"

"Did I? I am not at all droll now; I shall not often make you laugh now."

"Oh yes, I am sure you will; you were always so droll."

The subject of Mrs. Bligh's deceased waggeries seems about to drop, without any other being quite ready to take its place, which the author of those dead jokes feeling, makes an awkward snatch—not literally, but figuratively—at the tall little girl, as a new theme.

"And this is Sue? You see, I know all about you."

"And this is Fezy," replies the child, not nearly so much embarrassed as the stranger, and indicating a tiny coal-black muzzle tucked under her arm, from which are proceeding such ear-piercing yaps as could issue only from the mouth of a Spitz.

"Poor Lucile is in bed."

"Yes; how annoying! the coster's cart"—smiling intelligently—"Mr. Mulholland told us."

"Mr. Mulholland!" cries the hostess in a key of acute disappointment, as of one forestalled in the exhibition of some choice rarity. "Do you mean—is it possible that you have

seen Czar already? Did he," turning towards Pamela, "meet you at the station?"

"I do not think his name was Czar; I
think it was George."

"Oh, only George!" with an air of relief;
"I thought you could not have seen Czar."

"If I have, it is without knowing it. I
am afraid that I do not quite know who Czar
is."

"Oh, do not you? Of course not; how
stupid of me! Czar is my husband. We
always call him Czar; he will be in immediately; he is most anxious to make your
acquaintance. I am sure you and he will
get on. I am quite looking forward to hearing how you will draw each other out. Ah!
you may deny it, but you always were so
amusing. As for you, Pamela dear," again
turning towards the girl, with a laugh, "you
will be nowhere now, not in the running at
all."

One would think that so harmless, if flat a
pleasantry, would call for an answering word
or smile from a civil visitor, but in Miss Capel-

Smith it produces neither. It would seem doubtful, indeed, whether she heard it, so much occupied is she in explaining who she is to Fezy, who is still struggling madly to wriggle backwards from out the prison of his young mistress's elbow.

" I am always so glad that he should have anyone clever and brilliant to talk to," continues Mrs. Mulholland. " He is so thrown away here. I expect it will be a real treat to hear you two together. Oh, come now, no false modesty ; you know you always were considered one of the show girls at Madame Reybaud's."

" But indeed, indeed," very earnestly, " I am far from being a show woman now."

" Well, we shall judge about that," returns the hostess, with knowing confidence, adding, " I wonder Czar is not in by now ; I assure you that he was quite excited about you."

" I am very sorry to hear it," ruefully ; " someone has just passed the window, perhaps that was he. But it looked like quite a young man."

"Quite a young man!" echoes the wife delightedly. "I will tell him what you say. Well, he does look absurdly boyish. I tell him that I am sure I am often taken for his mother."

As she speaks the door opens briskly. and a man's jaunty figure comes in. At the first glance Anne has a recurrence of her first impression of the youthfulness of that figure ; and it is not till he has drawn quite near her that she becomes aware of the unlikely chestnut colour of his close curls, and of the fine network of little veins and wrinkles that go to make up the florid old face wreathed into so many smiles to greet her. Mrs. Bligh stands up shyly and holds out her hand ; while Mrs. Mulholland cries out in a voice of delighted expectation of all the brilliancies certain to follow upon the introduction :

"Czar, this is Nan! — Nan, this is Czar !"

"Will Mrs. Nan allow me to lay myself at her feet ?" says the old gentleman, bowing over her hand. "I hope your friend Char has told you how much we are in your debt for consenting to shine upon our darkness!"

"I have left you to make the pretty speeches," replies his wife, with an admiring smile ; "I know that you will do it so much better than I could!"

"We will do our best to amuse you ; but," with a shrug, "I am afraid we shall have to ask you to be lenient! As you see, we are a set of country bumpkins!"

He pauses, evidently to give an opportunity for the contradiction, which the person addressed is perfectly incapable of uttering. Seldom in her life has she been made to feel shyer than she is now by the florid amenities offered her, and by the consciousness that the friend of her childhood is awaiting with confident expectation the cascade of conversational fireworks which she knows herself to be so perfectly unable to let off.

"We have not much in the way of neighbours," continues Mr. Mulholland, with, as she fancies it, some slight diminution of expansiveness at her unresponsive silence ; "of course, excepting the Lascelles. They are in one's own *monde*, and one naturally knows where to have them ; but as for the rest, they are very good humdrum bodies in their way ; but——" with another shrug.

She hears herself saying something trite to the effect that country neighbours are apt to be not very amusing, and he assents.

" I agree—I perfectly agree with you ; but between you and me, when one gets below the *grand monde*, political or social, one is apt to find people everywhere a little provincial, do not you think so ?"

" I am afraid," with a dry smile, " that I am scarcely a judge ; not many of the *grand monde* find their way to Tite Street !"

" Ah ! you live in Tite Street, a name of doubtful omen, is not it ?" facetiously. " A good many people live in Tite Street. Ha, ha !"

His wife breaks into a hearty laugh at this speech, but seeing with some surprise, as Anne feels, that the latter echoes her mirth but faintly, hastens to say civilly :

" I am so little in London that I do not know Tite Street; but Pamela has told me that Chelsea is the height of the fashion, and that you have made your house exceedingly pretty—have not you, Pamela? Why, where is she?" looking in surprise round the room. " She has fled! Oh, no doubt Sue has taken her to see Lucile! Will you come and see poor Lucile? Though she is in bed, it is a shame that she should have to miss all the good things that I know we may expect from you two," glancing affectionately from one to the other.

" Then I am not to be banished? I am to be admitted?"

His wife giving him an eager permission to accompany them, he walks rather more springily than if he were eighteen to open the door for them, and they all file out.

CHAPTER V.

Miss Mulholland lies in bed, a pattern of vigorous English bloom, but she has by no means a monopoly of her couch of sickness. Pamela sits on one of her pillows, and George on the other. Sue is stretched all along the side of the mattress, with two very long black silk legs kicking up in the air; while to obviate any danger that may yet remain of the invalid's feeling lonely, a couple of dogs—a short-tempered lady of the sheep-dog kind, and a broken-haired white terrier—are having a friendly scrimmage across her prostrate body. With their mouths wide open, and showing all their beautiful clean teeth, they are apparently taking large mouthfuls out of each other's ears. At the entrance of the visitor, however, they cheerfully break off their gallantries in order to jump down from the bed and "make for her"—a proceeding which, if it has no other advantage, has at least that of taking off the stiffness of a first introduction, leading, as it does, to eager assurances on the part of the young owner that the bristled backs and rude voices mean nothing ; and counter-assurances on the stranger's side that she is not at all frightened, that she has dogs of her own, etc., etc. The ice is still further broken by Mr. Mulholland, who, having lingered behind the others, now pounces playfully out from behind the door, and is greeted by his daughter with a cry of surprise and joy that shows that his visits to the sick-room are not frequent occurrences.

"Czar, is that you? how awfully, awfully good of you!"

His response is to ask playfully whether she has room for one more, and getting a delighted assent, sits down on her bed, the dogs also having leapt back thither and resumed their tussle.

"I have not often seen an odder regimen for an invalid!"

"Ah, now you are beginning!" cries Mrs. Mulholland triumphantly; "that is just the dry voice in which you used to say things at Madame Reybaud's. Dear me, how it takes me back! do go on!"

"She likes us all to sit upon her—do not you, Luce?" breaks in Pamela, hurrying to the rescue, as she sees the consternation painted on Mrs. Bligh's face at this command to be funny. "We can't be too thick on the ground, can we?"

"She had the donkey up one day," cries Sue; "we had such difficulty in getting him upstairs; and he was so spiteful, he kicked out one of Fezy's front teeth."

"That was not an amiable trait," replies Anne; and then, in terror of being accused of dryness, adds hastily: "Was that the same donkey who behaved so ill in the tandem?"

" Oh no, that was the new one ; he is very ill-natured, too, but this was the old one, the one that Pamela and George always drive in the coster's cart."

At this innocent and matter-of-fact implication of an intimacy more developed than she had suspected between her young disciple and the person whom she herself had stigmatized as " a dreadful bore," Anne steals a guilty glance at Miss Capel-Smith in time to see with what a vexed flush the words " I believe I did drive him once or twice !" are accompanied.

" *Once or twice !*" repeats the little girl, in guileless astonishment. " Why, Pamela, what are you thinking of? have you forgotten? When last you were here, you and George were never out of the coster's cart, were you, George ?"

But George has arisen from his easy lounge on his sister's bolster, and calling to his terrier to accompany him, is stalking—an image of wounded feeling—to the door.

" He has gone to dress !" says Mrs. Mul-

6

holland, placid and unsuspecting; "we had better follow his example. Do not make yourself very splendid" (as she leads the way along the passage); "for, as you see, we are quite a family party. No outsider, except Pamela, and she" (affectionately) "is not an outsider; she is one of the family."

"I am nothing of the kind," says Pamela, in a mouthing whisper behind her hostess's back, to Mrs. Bligh. "You" (with a spasmodic grateful squeeze of the hand nearest to her) "have for ever saved me from that!"

Gratitude is a beautiful thing, and it is very delightful to have inspired it when one feels it is really merited; but Anne has not that happy consciousness, and she draws away her fingers.

Three-quarters of an hour later she is sitting at a well-be-lit and be-blossomed dinner-table at her host's right hand, and thinking that though she has made up her mind that she does not much like Mr. Mulholland, and that she wishes he would not call her "Mrs. Nan," yet that family life is a pleasant thing, and that if she could be quite sure that the look of expectancy of *bons mots* from herself, that never come, had departed out of Char's mild eyes, she would be quite enjoying herself.

Miss Capel-Smith is seated on the host's left hand, but, though the arrangement is a natural one, since there is no other lady, yet Anne is conscious that it has not been made without difficulty. She is almost certain of having heard coming from behind her, as they all entered the dining-room, an urgent remonstrance in Mrs. Mulholland's voice, addressed to somebody. "Pamela! what are you thinking of? Of course you will sit by Czar! you know he likes to have you." On the girl's other side the injured George has placed himself; and it is not without a vexed entertainment that Anne throughout dinner watches her votary's efforts to do the impossible, and turn a shoulder and a lump of rust-coloured hair at the same time impartially upon both her neighbours. Mrs. Bligh's own right hand is guarded by a person whom she incidentally learns to be staying in the house for the purpose of cataloguing the library. He is an under-bred, forward young man, who, though never spontaneously spoken to by anyone, interpellates each one in turn with vulgar familiarity, and takes all the fun and jokes as if addressed to himself.

"And how are we to entertain Mrs. Nan now that we have got her?" asks the host in a sprightly voice, looking up from a land-rail which has just been placed before him, and no duplicate of which has been offered to any other member of the company, a fact which Anne notes with surprise, though she had already observed his being supplied with a special and private vintage. "What are we to do for Mrs. Nan?" he repeats, as she does not answer; "shall we send her out for a blow in the lifeboat? or swing her up the side of a cliff to the quarries? or——"

"Anything on dry land!" she interrupts, smiling; "but as to watery pleasures——"

"You prefer terra-cotta, as Mrs. L—— said!" pausing to give his family time to

laugh at this fine crusted old jest. "Well,
then, terra-cotta it shall be!"

"I dare say the Lascelles will propose
something," says Mrs. Mulholland cheerfully; "I am sure that they are dying to see
you! I gave them such a glowing descrip-
tion of you; told them, how amu——"

"I do not know what you would do without the Lascelles," cries Pamela, rushing in
to hinder the dreaded accusation from again
issuing from the well-meaning lips that so
persistently frame it.

"And if you asked the Lascelles," replies
the old gentleman, taking up the remark,
"perhaps you might hear them say that
they did not quite know what they would
do without *us*."

"Without *us*," repeats his wife, with a
protesting accent. "It is very civil of you
to put it in the plural; but we will not
quarrel over *who* is the attraction" (with a
meaning smile); "they really are very kind
neighbours to us all, when they are down
here; and they are down a good deal!"

"And are you down here a good deal?"

There is a slight pause before the answer comes:

"Oh, we do not move much; we are very happy at home. Of course, Czar goes up now and again, naturally; but we do not stir much, it is such a business moving a whole household so great a distance."

"I take little bachelor trips up every now and then," says the old gentleman, with a shrug; "just to look in at the clubs, and knock up a few old cronies; and put in an appearance at a ball or two, to see how my former flames are wearing!"

"I do not suppose that the ladies thank you much for that!" says the vulgar young man, chuckling; but nobody takes the slightest notice of him or his remark.

"This is really too nice!" cries Mrs. Mulholland, with a fresh access of good-natured expansiveness, as the two ladies stand *tête-à-tête* over the drawing-room fire. "That I should be having 'little Nan' under my own roof! You were short of your age, do you recollect? and you were so afraid that you were going to be a dwarf! Do you remember? It was always a promise that you should stay with me when I married. How little I thought then " (looking upwards with fervent and unaffected gratitude) "what happiness was in store for me!"

"And you really are very happy?" asks Anne, hoping that her own tones do not sound as incredulous to her friend as they do to herself.

The wife answers by a rapturous smile:

"You see how brilliant he is! and he is always like that, always, always, even when we are quite alone! except when he gets out of spirits from having been here too long, and then I send him up to London. Of course, it would be most unjustifiable to keep him vegetating here always, and so we live rather quietly all the year round—we are not very well off--so that he may do his little jaunts comfortably in the season."

"What an unselfish woman you must be!"

She would have liked to have exchanged

this exclamation for its converse—" What a selfish old pig he must be !" but she refrains.

" Unselfish !" (with a surprised accent); "oh ! because I have to lose his society for so long ; but then I know he is enjoying himself. He pretends he does not, but I know that he does. Of course he is made immensely much of in London ; and we all like to be made much of ; and the children and I are very happy together here. It is one of my many blessings that his children like me. Ah, Czar, here you are!" as the subject of her encomiums, having finished his special bottle, and grown tired of his son's and the librarian's company, now joins them. " We were talking of you. Listeners never hear any good of themselves, you know," smiling at the excellence of the joke. " Come and sit by Nan, and amuse her."

The old gentleman at once complies with the first half of the request, sliding his jaunty body into an armchair at his guest's side ; but with the latter half it is—little as he suspects it—quite out of his power to comply; and though he asks leave to call her Nan, *tout court*, and playfully threatens never to answer her unless she addresses him as "Czar," she feels that it is with a guilty flatness that she responds to his wife's appeal as they part for the night:

" He *is* brilliant, is not he ?"

"Oh yes, very!" answers she baldly; "and" (laughing awkwardly) "I hope you are now quite disabused of that painful and most erroneous idea that I am brilliant too."

"You are tired to-night," replies Char, with amiable evasiveness; "but" (shaking her head) "I have not altered my opinion; it is there still. It will come out to-morrow." Reiterating that "it is there still," and pursued by anguished assurances from her visitor that it is not, Mrs. Mulholland retires smiling.

*   *   *   *   *

"Yes, it is all very fine, and of course I am the gainer," says Mrs. Bligh next morning after breakfast, as she and Pamela walk

through the climbing wood that backs the
house to reach the barer hill beyond the
view. " But what I wish to arrive at is why
you are not at this moment in the coster's
cart, of which I overheard at breakfast an
almost tearful proffer being made you."

The girl makes no answer beyond a slight
grimace. Under the trees the Lent lilies
are strewn broadcast, and about their feet
are the creeping ivy and the hyacinth shoots
—all the delightful flooring of an early spring
wood—while through the riot of wild garlic
that has the impudence to look like lily of the
valley, the dogs scampering after a hare
make it, by bruising its leaves, disclose its
true nature.

" According to Sue, last time you were
here you were never out of the coster's cart."

" I had nothing better to do. I had not
you ; now that I have you——" (rapturously).

" Oh yes " (hastily), " I understand ! or,
rather " (laughing), " I do not understand !"

" I suppose," says Pamela thoughtfully,
"that one outgrows people as one outgrew

one's clothes when one was a child. I think I have outgrown George."

" How long ago ?" (in a tone whose dryness would have satisfied even Mrs. Mulholland)— "twenty-four hours ?"

Miss Capel-Smith does not answer this sarcastic question, but pursues her own line of thought.

" When one has been used to people all one's life, I suppose that one is apt to take them for granted ; to accept them as one accepts one's self. One no more thinks of criticising them than one thinks of criticising one's parents, and then some fine day a lanthorn is turned upon them, perhaps by some careless remark, uttered by a person whose opinion one has every reason to value, and one sees them from henceforth in their true colours."

" And no doubt," says Anne, with a laugh of sincere vexation, " one fine day some blabbing fool will casually observe to you that I am ' a dreadful bore,' and I shall go to the wall too."

The girl breaks out into eager protestation, " Oh, *you !* as if there were the slightest parallel ; as if there were the remotest possibility ; but " (slowly) " do not you think that one's standard may change ? that when one's experience is larger, and one gets a glimpse of what a man ought to be——"

" And where have you been getting these glimpses ?" asks Mrs. Bligh with a sudden disagreeable fear of she knows not what. " Where have you been meeting these giants by whom you are going to measure poor humanity ?"

" Oh, nowhere !" answers the girl, in innocent surprise at the sharpness of her companion's tone. " You know all my acquaintances—how humdrum they are ! I have not met anybody in the least interesting all the winter except——"

But for some perverse and inscrutable reason the widow is resolved not to hear the name of the exception, and she breaks in with an abrupt remark about the scenery. They have outclimbed the wood, and are standing in the close winter grass of the hillside which the sheep are cropping, and where the long-tailed lambs are skipping over their mothers' backs, and leaping in the air with all four legs off the ground at once; one engaging black one, like a little dog, seems leader of their artless games. Out of unnumbered small brown buds the liberal gorse flowers are already profusely bursting, their sweetness guarded by fierce green spikes. Below, the trees of the wood they have just left are purpling against the sea, and against the bright, cold, lovely sky.

"What a piece of luck it is for me!" exclaims Pamela, "that that old——that Mr. Mulholland keeps his wife running on his errands all the forenoon, else I should never have had a chance of asking you what you think of them all. Did I give you a good idea of them—of Mrs. Mulholland, for instance ?"

Anne laughs again, and much more naturally than last time.

"I still fail to see why she is 'splunchy.'"

"And Sue?"

"She is an undoubted 'ripper'!"

"And Lucile?"

"I dare say she is a ripper, too; she looked like one, as far as I could judge from the very little I could see of her, under the two dogs and six people who were sitting upon her!"

"And Mr. Mulholland?"

They both pause in their walk, and face each other. There is mirth as well as inquiry in the younger woman's red-brown eyes—a mirth so catching that it is reflected in Anne's.

"I am not going to be inveigled into sarcasms on my host," she answers; but her voice is unsteady with laughter as she speaks. "He is a very nice, civil-spoken old gentleman; and, indeed, my dear child" (more gravely), "as he is our host, you might be a little polite to him."

For a moment or two it seems as though Pamela were going to receive this remonstrance in silence, and they both look down

at the wood beneath them, where the still
wintry trees have a sort of uneasy look about
them ; no hint of green yet, but the feeling
of all the great leaves encased in the little
compass of the restless buds.   Then—

"Would you be polite to a person who
was always trying to kiss you on the stairs ?"
asks the girl slowly.

" I really cannot face so unlikely a con-
tingency," answers Anne, taken aback.
" But do you mean—is it possible——"

" He lies in wait for me on the landing ;
he pounces out on me from behind doors ;
he tries to squeeze my fingers when I hand
him his teacup at breakfast," replies the girl
tragically.   " I think I had better warn you,
lest he should attempt anything of the same
kind with you."

" I do not think that in my case there is
much danger," answers Mrs. Bligh, mentally
contrasting the homeliness of her own appearance, of which she is at all times perhaps
exaggeratedly conscious, with the exquisite
porcelain texture, the fire and dew and

carmine of the young face before her. " But does Char—does his wife——"

" I think she suspects it, and she does not like it, poor dear!"— with an accent of disgust—"she can't like it less than I do! One day I asked him whether he had ever read Thackeray's 'Mrs. Perkins's Ball,' and whether he had ever met those three attractive old gentlemen— Lord Tarquin, Lord Methusaleh, Lord Billy Goat. He was so angry!"

" That was not very surprising."

" And yet she does not like me to snub him, either," continues the girl, with a wondering intonation. " Sweet as her temper is, I have seen her quite put out because she thought I did not wish to sit by him. Good heavens!" — with an accent of excessive impatience—" what a horrible thing a love like that is—a love that degrades! How earnestly one must hope that when one's hour comes one will love up, and not down!"

CHAPTER VI.

" WELL, and how has Mrs. Nan enjoyed
her constitutional?" asks the host, one of
whose methods of getting on his guest's
nerves is by speaking of her in the third
person; and when they are all gathered
round the luncheon-table a couple of hours
later: "I was a little hurt at not being
invited to join the party; but you were quite
right — quite right! A pair of young
members of the Alpine Club like you would
soon have distanced such a poor old cripple
as I!"

He pauses to give time for the mirth that
must follow upon this picture of his infirmities,
adding, when the proper dues of merriment

7

have been paid, " Come here, Miss Pamela,"
patting the seat of a chair beside him, "and
give an account of yourself. How have you
been entertaining Mrs. Nan ?"

" We went up the hill," replies Pamela ;
but perhaps in deference to her friend's
remonstrance accepting the seat offered with
less overt rebellion than usual.

" And what did you talk about ? From
the little I know of young ladies I do not
think two of them are likely to walk along
together in total silence—ha ! ha ! Did you
discuss us ? I feel sure " (playfully) " that
Mrs. Nan was very cynical, and picked us
all to pieces."

" I am not at all afraid," replies his wife,
looking round with a benevolent confidence,
that makes both feel rather guilty, at the
two visitors—" not at all afraid of trusting
our characters in either of their hands."

" I am not so sure of that. I should
like to have been eavesdropping behind
one of our stone walls as you passed
—eh ?"

" Perhaps it is as well that you were not,"
replies Anne daringly, and acting on the
maxim that if you wish to deceive a person
the easiest and surest way is to tell the exact
truth. " We said some very terrible things
of you !"

They all laugh heartily at the excellence of
this joke, Pamela seeming peculiarly tickled
by it ; and then there is a lull, while kind-
hearted little Sue, quite oblivious of her own
dinner, gallops round the table in eager
attention to everyone's wants ; while the
vulgar young man, with officious assiduity,
presses the family's own food upon it, addressing the younger members with low-bred ease
by their Christian names.

" May I ask, Char, what your plans for the
afternoon are ?" inquires the old gentleman
presently, pouring himself out a glass of what
Anne, though perfectly ignorant of wines,
divines to be some costly fluid. " I send the
servants away ; do not you think I am quite
right ? Is not it hard "—seeing Mrs. Bligh's.
eyes involuntarily fixed on his glass — " that

I can't get anyone to help me with my Château Margaux ? Char, I say, what are your plans for the afternoon ?"

" I thought of taking Nan out in the victoria, and, of course, it would be very pleasant for Pamela if you felt inclined to drive her out in your buggy."

Anne looks at her friend while she is making this speech, and, enlightened by her disciple's confidences of the forenoon, has no difficulty in interpreting the dual anxiety indicated on the dial-plate of her good-natured face. A double and almost contra-dictory anxiety that her proposal should not be jumped at too eagerly by one of the parties concerned in it was rejected with too much energy by the other.

" I am afraid I have a pre-engagement," replies Pamela precipitately ; for, being between the devil and the deep sea, she hastens to throw herself into the embrace of the latter. " I believe I am to go out with George in the coster's cart. I do not think he would like me to throw him over—only where is he ?" seeming to become aware for the first time that his place is empty.

"Oh, how sorry he will be!" cries Sue, her brother's stanch little bottle-holder and semi-confidant. "He thought you did not want him, as you would not go out with him this morning. So he has taken his gun and gone to look for a snipe. He said he would not be back till near dinner.'

There is an awkward pause, broken by the young vulgarian saying jocosely, "I am afraid your coster's cart does not look very healthy," and by Mr. Mulholland observing in a resentful tone, "And I am afraid that, failing the young gentleman, you will have to put up with the old one."

The situation is so strained, that everyone is relieved when a diversion is made by the entry of a servant with a note for Mrs. Mulholland, which she at once opens, and having read, gives utterance to an exclamation of disappointment.

"How provoking! I beg your pardon, Nan, but I asked the Lascelles to dinner for

to-morrow to meet you, and they can't come.
Did not you understand, Czar, that they
were not going to have an Easter party this
year ? But it seems they are expecting a
man. Lady Lascelles mentions him as if I
ought to know who he is, but I never heard
of him before to my knowledge—Sir Robert
Coke !" (pronouncing his name as it is spelt).

"Cook, my dear ! Cook !" cries her
husband, correcting her pronunciation with
as excruciated an air as a musician who hears
a false note struck. " Sir Robert Coke the
sculptor ; why, of course, we all know him !
I met him at Marlborough House last year.
If my memory does not fail me, H.R.H.
himself did me the honour of presenting him
to me. I remember that I talked to him
about Marochetti."

Sir Robert Coke ! For the first moment
or two after the piece of news thus conveyed
falls upon her ear, Anne does not look up
from the cold tan muzzle which Lassie, the
sheep-dog, has just laid on her knee, with a
little knock to hint that she is quite willing

to share in any of the refreshments that are
going. A repetition of the uttered name, in
a tone of stifled ecstasy from the other side
of the table, makes her lift her eyes, to meet
those of Pamela shooting a red fire of delight
across at her, while a vivid flash of pleasure
heightens the already remarkable beauty of
her colouring.

"Good heavens!" (the reflection comes
with a quick shock); the girl is as pleased at
the tidings as she herself is, or was, a
moment ago. And though reason hastens to
assure her that it is on her account that her
votary is so elated, though memory recalls to
her how keenly the girl has identified herself
with her joys and sorrows from the beginning
of their acquaintance, yet she mislikes the
colour which is the flag that her joy hangs out
quite as much as Lancelot did poor Elaine's.

"Why not ask them to bring him with
them?" suggests the host, after having read
the note, which has been passed down the
table to him. "I dare say they would be
glad to show him that they have neighbours

who speak some language beside Welsh ;
and you need not be nervous, my dear ; he
is perfectly *comme il faut.*"

"Oh, I do not doubt it ! The Lascelles
never have anybody who is not nice ; and
naturally, if you met him at Marlborough
House——"

"Of course" (with a shrug), "in my young
days—I mean" (correcting himself) "a very
few years ago— a man who makes faces and
busts—ha ! ha !—was not precisely the person
whom one would invite to sit down to dinner
with one, but *tempora mutantur ;* and we
have all of us the highest example for taking
Bohemia by the hand."

Miss Capel-Smith laughs derisively.

"Do you call Sir Robert Coke Bohemia ?"

This remark brings down a shower of
questions upon its utterer.

"Do you know him ?"

"Is he a friend of yours ?"

"He is not a friend of *mine,*" with a very
slight accent on the pronoun, and as slight a
glance of intelligence thrown across to her

friend ; " but I was once taken to his studio."

" Was he nice ?   Did you like him ?"

" He was extremely, remarkably nice to me ; but that was because—that was not———"

Again she glances across the table, but the answering look she receives makes her abandon any intention she may have nourished of explaining that the civilities paid her were vicarious ones.

" I must look in on him, if I have a spare half-hour, next time I am up !" says the host patronizingly.   " I am told that he has been doing some cleverish things."

" If you know him, Pamela, that is an additional reason for asking him," says Mrs. Mulholland.   " We will put you next him at dinner ; it will be much pleasanter for him than finding himself among such a set of total strangers as we all are, will not it, Nan ?   Is the messenger gone ?   Ring and ask, and I will write at once."

" Was there ever anything so exciting ?" cries Pamela, the moment that she and Mrs.

Bligh are alone, thrusting her arm excitedly through the widow's, as they both pass along the corridor to pay the invalid Lucile a visit. "To think of his having put aside all his work—he whose whole heart and soul seems bound up in it—to come posting down after you ; and these dear idiots "—with a chuckle of exquisite amusement—"quite making up their minds that he is my friend ! What a delicious mystification ! It is almost a pity that we cannot keep it up a little !"

Anne is saved from the embarrassment of either assenting to or dissenting from this suggestion, by their having reached Lucile's room. Miss Mulholland is convalescent, and lying on a sofa, surrounded by drawing-boards, paint-brushes, and oil-colours, and with a spirited little oil sketch of two horses pulling hay out of a manger on a small easel before her. At her feet sits Sue, grasping her adored Fezy in her arms.

"We must show Sir Robert Coke these, must not we ?" says Pamela, picking up one of the scattered drawings. " I dare say he

will give you an introduction to the President
of the Blank Exhibition. I am sure he is
much too clever not to see how clever they
are. I prophesy"--joyously—"that he will
take a particular fancy to this !"—indicating
one.

" I hope he will not take a particular fancy
to Fezy !" cries Sue apprehensively, and
hugging the little inky *chef d'œuvre* to her
breast. " If he asks me for him, I shall
answer " — assuming a very tragic and
dramatic air—"' I will give you the skin
off my back, but I will not give you Fezy.' "

Her sister laughs.

" You know you are so fond of planning
long high-flown speeches, which you are
never able to deliver when the time comes.
Now, Sue, tell the truth : if you had to give
up me or Fezy, which would it be ?"

Sue hesitates.

" Of course "—reluctantly—" I suppose
I should have to keep you, but I should go
and hang myself at once !"

" Oh yes, I know "—derisively—" you

would go and hang yourself just opposite the
hall-door, where someone would be sure to
come and cut you down.   But "—with a
change of key from this light banter to one
of serious interest—" do you really think
that so great a swell would care to look at
my sketches?   Sometimes, I know, the
bigger the swell, the kinder.   It is often
only the small swells that give themselves
airs, and as he is a friend of yours, you would
be sure to know.   He is a friend, isn't
he ?"

"Oh, a devoted friend!" replies Pamela,
her eyes sparkling.   "He worships the
ground I tread on.   Is not he coming all
the way to Anglesey to tell me so ?"

"Is he really?" cries Sue in an awed
tone, while Lucile adds : "You had better
not say anything before Sue that you do
not want taken literally.   She is as green
as grass !"

Anne has picked up another of the strewn
drawings, and is scrutinizing it with an
apparently close attention, of which she is

not aware, until roused by the voice of the young artist.

"Oh, do not look at that one; the mare is not so bad, but Czar is wretched. It does not give any idea of his charm."

Anne thinks that it would be very odd if it did, but she only says:

" Why do you call him Czar ?"

" He does not like the word 'father '; at least, he does not like us to call him father before people; and you know the Russians call their Emperor ' Little Father,' so he asked us would we mind calling him Czar."

" I see." In point of fact, Mrs. Bligh is unconscious of what the object before her is intended to represent, with such absent eyes is she regarding it, while through her mind there passes the reflection that it is ungrateful not to be diverted by a jest, invented wholly for your amusement, and that yet Pamela's mystification seems to her singularly wanting in the element of humour. She must be a better actress, however, than she has ever before had reason to suppose herself; since, in happy ignorance of her lack of appreciation of any joke, her young admirer carries it on with unflagging spirit, and with frequent glances of delighted intelligence at herself throughout the rest of that and the whole of the ensuing day ; nor is the expected stranger ever mentioned by any member of the family —and in a household not very rich in events it occurs somewhat frequently—without the prefix of " Pamela's friend."

" It seems hardly worth while writing the names of so small a party," says Mrs. Mulholland, ambling round the dinner-table on the afternoon of the next day with some strips of paper in her hand. " But I always think it is safer, do not you, Nan ? People are sure to shuffle themselves badly if you leave it to themselves."

" Oh, Czar, which is to take me in, Sir Thomas or Sir Robert ? They are both baronets."

" My dear child, I blush for you," returns Czar, pulling her ear affectedly. " The Lascelles' creation dates from 1660, while our

poor Coke is a mere unknown, a toadstool—
a toadstool of genius, I grant you—ha! ha!
—but still a toadstool!"

"Then Sir Robert must take Nan," says
the hostess, picking out the two names from
her little bundle. "But then how shall we
manage to put Pamela near him?"

"He will have to bridle his impatience till
after dinner," replies the old gentleman, with
a rather spiteful smile; "and in the meanwhile they must content themselves with
sighing and ogling."

"Ogling!" repeats Pamela, bursting into a
laugh. "What a dear old-fashioned word!
Did people ogle in your young days, Mr.
Mulholland? Yes, if you put him opposite
to me, he can gaze his fill. Some people
think it an even better position than being by
the side of the adored object."

As Mrs. Bligh dresses for dinner, with an
earliness that has a touch of the feverish in it,
one of her causes of hesitating self-congratulation is, that a period will now surely soon
be put to Miss Capel-Smith's rather tiresome

joke. She finds in the drawing-room only
her hostess, who greets her with an exclamation of genuine surprise that sounds very
pleasantly in her ears.

" Nan, what a metamorphosis ! Well, you
do pay for dressing, as they say. Come to
the light, and let me have a good look at you.
I remember at Madame Reybaud's they used
to laugh at me, but I always said you had
great possibilities. What a charming gown,
and what a delightful pendant ! Old, of
course. How pretty the little enamel ribbon
tying together the two diamond hearts ! Ah,
of course !"— changing her tone to a more
subdued one, befitting the lugubrious theme
—"poor Colonel Bligh's hair ; reddish, was
it ? I always imagined him a dark man.
Czar, come here and admire Nan ! Why,
Pamela, you *have* made yourself smart.
Ah, we all know why !" laughing signifi-
cantly.

The old gentleman advances alertly,
odorous with white rose.

" I am dazzled," he says, in his usual strain

of florid compliment, putting up his hand to his eyes. " Char, give me a shade !"

" Sir Thomas and Lady Lascelles, and Sir Robert Coke," announces the butler ; and " Ah, Milady !" cries the host, " punctual to the moment, and in such a frock ! I see "— repeating his simulation of bedazzlement— " you are determined to blind a poor old fellow."

The two ladies exchange civil " So good of you to come !" and " So good of you to ask us !" And then it is Anne's turn to be affectionately presented as " My dear old school-friend, the one I have so often told you about, who always used to make us laugh so."

The subject of this kindly little memoir would have been glad to have had the last clause of the sentence omitted ; but she responds to the easy politenesses that the introduction calls forth with such composure as is left her by the consciousness that the sculptor, with his bright dark eyes flashing under his beautiful thick gray hair, is at her elbow, waiting his moment to claim her attention. To-day, at least, she can accuse him of no laggardness in greeting her.

The clasp of his hand, at once prompt and lingering, speaks his real pleasure in the meeting, and in his face she reads a far pleasanter version of the surprised approbation of her temporary good looks but lately expressed with so much *naïveté* by Char.

There is as distinct an effort to isolate himself and her from the rest of the party as is compatible with his perfect good breeding—and oh, crowning mercy! his eye has lit carelessly on Pamela, without any apparent consciousness of having ever before seen her. These various sources of comfort enable Mrs. Bligh to bear with calmness the breaking into Coke's first sentence to her of the old host, with :

" Last time we met was under the roof of our future king—ha! ha! If you remember. I was fortunate enough to interest you by telling you some traits of Marochetti, etc.," and she addresses to herself a paraphrase of the consolation offered by Dryden to Mrs. Anne Killigrew—" Heaven's eternal year is thine." The dinner-hour, though, alas! far from eternal, will be hers.

CHAPTER VII.

"The shepherd, nipt with bitter winter's rage,
  Frolics not more to see the painted spring
  Than I do to behold your majesty."

"BLESS that dear old gentleman for giving
you to me!" says the sculptor, gently pressing the hand on his arm against his side,
as he leads Anne to the dining-room; "what
a delightful face he has!"

"DELIGHTFUL!"

"Yes: it is so like old Nellie, the ourang-
outang's, at the Zoo. You never go to the
Zoo? Ah! you must let me take you there,
and we will stroke the gazelles' wet black
noses, and laugh at the odd gawky birds
together."

"You are so likely to have time!" she

answers, with an abrupt yet blissful laugh. "I think," guiding him to the spot where she had seen Mrs. Mulholland regretfully deposit his name—regretfully, since it is at a distance from his supposed favourite—in the afternoon; "I think we are here."

There is the usual little noise of pulling in chairs and settling skirts, and Coke naturally casts a glance round the table, in order to make the arrangements of which easier, and also because the master of the house thinks it more genteel, he and his wife face each other at the sides; while Mrs. Bligh and the young librarian occupy the two most prominent positions of head and foot. From her point of vantage, Anne can command the expression of each of the eight faces round her; and can, since the table corner interposes between them, make surreptitious observations on her neighbour's countenance with more ease than if she were alongside of him. Surely now that Miss Capel-Smith is full in his eye on the host's left hand, and now that table decorations

creep instead of soaring, he cannot fail to
recognise her.   But it so happens that just
as his eye takes its careless sweep round,
her head is averted, perhaps merely from
that tendency which seems inveterate in it
to present its back to " Czar," and Coke's
glance returns unenlightened, unexcited, and
contented to his own lady.

" Talking of time," she says, conscious
if yet quite unable to get rid of that ugly
brusqueness in her tone, " how did you get
time to come here ?   You assured me it was
a sheer impossibility !"

" Did not you tell me that you were going to
Anglesey ?" he asks ; then, seeing a hesitating
and too radiant credulity in her face, he adds
hastily : " What a terrible woman you are !
you are not only horribly honest yourself,
but you compel a habitually dishonest person
like me to be honest too !   I should never, no
never, have summoned up energy to come "
—seeing her face fall—" if I had not known
you were here ; but the truth is, I had another
motive.   I was told that this Welsh fellow

had a Porbus in his collection that I wanted to see. No, it is a fool's errand so far. He thinks it is a replica of the one at the Hague, but it is not. It is a copy, only I shall not undeceive him ; he would turn me out of the house " (laughing), "and give his mother's monument to the local stonemason, if I did."

" That would be a pity !" she says flatly ; and he, seeing perhaps a shadow of disappointment for which he is responsible lying on her features, cannot refrain from adding caressingly :

" I had such a long chilly journey to-day, that I think when first I saw the cold gray sea splashing the shore I should have turned back, if I had not had the thought to warm me that I should find a little friend at the end !"

" Did the Prince come to your studio on Monday ?" asks the little friend precipitately. Well as he knows her and her abruptness, it always gives him a cold douche.

" Monday ? yes, it was Monday."

"And Tuesday?" (recalling the engagements with which he had parried her un-
expressed wish for another sight of him
before her departure)—"did you go down
into the country and make more sketches of
Rayon d'Or ?"

" Did not I ?" answers he emphatically,
his whole face lighting up with an eager
delight, which, as she reflects, no thought
of her or relish of her society has ever been
able to call into it. " I had a glorious day
of it. I had him out into a meadow, and
ran by his side as he was trotting, galloping,
and sometimes rearing !"

" I should like to have been there."

" I promised the groom half a crown a
rear, and we did our best."

" It must have been tiring work, was
not it ?"

" Yes, of course, that kind of study does
take a good deal out of you, and the strain
upon eye and brain to catch a particular
instant, which shows how the four legs can
at one moment be in relation to each other,

is immense ; but "—with that recurring lighting of the eye—"it is a delightful kind of
fatigue! And how one sleeps after it! Like
a tired hound!"

Her intelligent face kindles with sympathetic interest, and yet a light pang shoots
through her. Is it possible that she is jealous
even of his work?

"You will be able to get on swimmingly
now, then," she says, with keen relish, "without any more of those hitches and delays
that have chafed you so much."

He sighs.

"No such luck! There are half a dozen
dead people between me and him. You
know I was telegraphed for last week to
take a cast of old Sir Peter Mammon. He
looked "—with a slight shudder of disgust—
"like a dead Silenus!"

Her cheek flushes indignantly.

"Why do you accept such work? Why
do not you leave dead brewers and live
aldermen to journeymen? You, who are
fortunate enough not to have a wife and

children to make degrading pot-boilers a
duty !"

" Fortunate !" he repeats in a tone of
melancholy, which for the moment he
believes to be perfectly genuine, though
there may possibly be in it a dash of what
in a woman would be called coquetry. " Do
you think me to be congratulated for having
struck no roots anywhere ?"

" What has become," she asks, shying
away from this vaguely agitating question,
" of the imaginative work that your heart
seemed so set upon, whose subject we so
often discussed in Dorsetshire ?"

He smiles with good-humoured indulgence
at her vehemence, thinking the while that
he wished she would get out of temper
oftener, since the effect is so greatly to
enhance her physical attractions.

" Did not I tell you that I was to do a fountain for old Lady ——— ?   I only accepted on
the condition that I should have *carte blanche*
as to subject and treatment.   Bless my soul !"
with a sudden change of tone, " *apropos*

of Lady ——, is not that the little dewy rose-
bud she brought to my studio last Sunday
—the little darling with whom I made such
friends by echoing her raptures over you ?"

The recognition, hitherto accidentally
delayed, but which was, of course, inevitable,
has come.

"What must she think of me for not
having known her before?" returning, with
what his friend thinks an unnecessary
empressement, the hesitating smile and bow,
lovely in their rosy shyness, which the young
girl throws him across the board. Not very
happily placed herself between the host and
the young vulgarian, she has been watching
with the deepest interest the two persons
on the opposite side of the table, and forming absorbed conjectures as to the subject
of their conversation from the motion of
their lips. "Did I ever know her name,
or have I forgotten it ?" asks Coke, in a low
voice, of his neighbour. "Tell me what it
is, but speak low, for she is pricking those
little shelly ears."

" Her name is Smith."

It would have been generous to add the graceful prefix of " Pamela." But there are moments when generosity is difficult.

" I wish she would sit for my Nereid," still surveying the girl with the openness of perfect innocence of heart. " I would put her on a sea-horse, with her dear little dimpled hands twisted in his mane." Then, seeing no particularly avid acceptance of this suggestion in the usually keenly sympathetic face of his neighbour, he adds more seriously : " Do you think, dear friend, that you can be more anxious for me, than I am for myself, to get away from Kensal Green into the upper air ? Do you think that I enjoy seeing my studio "—with a gesture of disgust—" fast becoming a necropolis ?"

" Then why do you let it ? Why do not you get away ?" asks she bluntly.

The question is, perhaps, not an easy one to answer, and her downright earnest eyes make him uncomfortable, for his reply is to change the subject.

" Ought not I "—lowering his voice—" to say something to the good lady on my right? She is my hostess, and though you "—with an affectionate smile—"have a way of making me forget everyone else when I am talking to you, yet I suppose I ought to say five words to her, oughtn't I ?"

" Of course you ought," answers she shortly, and instantly turns away her head, to show that she makes no further claim on his attention.

She can't avoid overhearing the rather nervous apology for not having placed him near his supposed intimate with which Mrs. Mulholland opens the conversation ; but in order to avoid catching his courteous, if rather puzzled, rejoinder, she herself rushes into talk with the sulky George, who, hitherto wholly neglected by her, now sits looking straight before him, eating his dinner in morose silence.

" Did you get many snipe ?"

" Only one."

" You had better "—conciliatingly—" have

stayed at home, and driven out Pamela in the coster's cart."

No answer.

" When you go out together, which drives, you or she? and do you stand up like real costers?"

" We sit down."

" How extremely well she is looking to-night !"

" Is she?" Then, casting a glance of resentful indifference in her direction, " I think her very much over-dressed."

Mrs. Bligh pauses, baffled, reflecting, a little cynically, how thankful she would have been if the angry young gentleman beside her had, on the occasion of Lady St. George's luncheon, treated her to his present irate silence. But being a good-hearted woman, conscious of having unintentionally done him an injury, and, strongest motive of all, being determined not, by looking neglected, to seem to claim a return of Coke's notice, she perseveres.

" You would not like her to come down

to dinner in a tweed tailor gown?" she asks, not because she supposes that he or any other living being could nourish so senseless a desire, but because she is resolved to keep saying something.

And before the tardy reply to her idiotic query can come, she hears a voice softly saying at the back of her head:

" I have done my duty. Come back to me!"

For the rest of dinner young Mr. Mulholland is at liberty to sulk at ease. . . .

" Well?" cries Pamela, in a voice of delighted expectation, sliding her arm under the widow's, and detaining her with gentle force in the hall before letting her enter the drawing-room after dinner.

" Well!" answers Anne, with an embarrassed laugh.

" I do not think I can keep up my mystification much longer, can I ?"—with a pleased chuckle. " Even they will see through it. What an interesting face he has! What a play of features! You had a delightful dinner."

" It is more than you had, I am afraid."

" Oh, I did not mind! The old Satyr "— with a grimace—" was happily too much occupied in subjugating Lady Lascelles to harry me; and I was quite, quite happy watching you two! Oh, of course "— anxiously—" I did not hear a word you said! I would not for worlds have tried! How determined he was "—again laughing delightedly—" that you should not waste any words upon that stupid George! and he was perfectly right. It would have been casting pearls before swine. Do you know "— growing grave—" I am afraid that George has not at all a nice nature; I think he is very vindictive."

" Poor George! I do not know why he visits your misdeeds upon me."

" I was thinking at dinner that I wondered why it had never struck me before what a very bad countenance he has!"

" Poor George! You know "—playfully— "love is always as unbecoming to a man as it is becoming to a woman."

"It is not unbecoming to some men," replies Pamela, with a significant shake of her lovely head; and though Anne is well aware that the state of mind alluded to has nothing in common with the relations between herself and the sculptor, yet the baseless implication quickens her pulses.

Perhaps the little effervescence of spirits produced by the suggestion helps her to bear the trial in store for her, when, upon the entry of the men, her host throws himself with juvenile agility on a *pouf* at her feet, declaring that, "whatever happens, Mrs. Nan must not be neglected;" while, with eyes at the back of her head, she sees the eager courtesy with which Sir Robert Coke is making his apologies to Pamela, and the rosy alacrity with which they are received.

But to-day Mrs. Bligh's star is in the ascendant, for whether or not nettled by the absence of manner with which she responds to his inquiries as to "who built that killing frock," the old gentleman swiftly springs with scarcely any difficulty to his little patent-leather-covered feet, and leaves her. And then—

" Is he coming back ?" asks a voice at her elbow.

" I hope not "—with a very slight smile.

" Then I may stay ; but, as I am not so young as he "—laughing—" I will not be so lowly "—choosing a higher chair. " They do not do anything here of an evening, I hope—no music or *petits jeux ?*"

" Nothing."

" Thank God ! Then we can talk."

She hitches her chair unconsciously a shade nearer his.

" Let us talk of your work."

" Let us "—with a shrug—" not talk of my work ! When you look through me with your gimlet eyes, and ask me in your trenchant voice when I am going to do something imaginative, you make me feel such a shabby fellow ; you make me blush for my pot-boilers ! I do not like feeling shabby ; I do not like blushing !"

She is silent.

"Now, if"—with a sigh—"I had some-one always at my elbow to pull me by the sleeve, and point me with her little emphatic forefinger to the stars, I might do some-thing—I do not say that it is likely—but I might."

She has dropped her eyes, conscious that they are growing mistful. Mrs. Bligh has not had much happiness in her life, and it has seemed to her that the sufferings which she has been called upon to bear have been of a kind to sour, and not ripen.

"If I only had time"—hitching his chair in turn nearer hers, and passing his hand through his hair—"I have an idea that I think would please my conscience. Do you know that I always to myself call you my conscience?"

"Do you?"

"It is the death of Pedasus. Now, you have not the least idea who Pedasus was. Do you know, madam, that you are very ignorant? Well, he was one of Achilles' horses. He had two immortal horses,

Xanthus and Balius ; but poor Pedasus was
only a mortal, like you or me, and so, though
he was a fine plucky fellow, Sarpedon ran
him through with his spear ; and as old
Chapman says — do you ever read old
Chapman ?—

> "as he joy'd to die
> By his so honourable hand, did even in dying neigh."

Do you like the idea ?" (leaning closely over
her in his eagerness) — "is it a good
moment ?"

"I am so sorry to interrupt you," strikes
in the soft, apologetic purr of their hostess ;
"I am sure you will hate me for breaking
into your comfortable talk, but "—turning to
Coke—"you must know that it is my little
girl's birthday, and it has been a long
promise that she should recite Gray's 'Bard.'
She has been learning it upon purpose,
and you will not be too hard upon her ; she
is only eleven years old," etc., etc.

They have both been so absorbed in their
topic that they are conscious of having almost

sprung apart when suddenly called back to the present.

"Perfidious woman!" says Coke, with an air of humorous resentment, as soon as Mrs. Mulholland's back is turned : "did not you swear to me that they did nothing ?"

"It is in honour of you," she answers, laughing, while a secret anxiety possesses her lest, the thread of their talk being so rudely broken, he should not care any longer to keep his place beside her. But he does, and not only his place, but his intimate attitude of leaning over the side of his arm-chair nearest to her, with his thoughtful head propped on his nervous artist-hand. It gives her a foolish glow to think how little he cares to conceal the evidences of his high friendship for her—a glow that lasts all through the performance, from Sue's excited rush at—

"Ruin seize thee, ruthless king !"

to the final—

"Deep in the roaring tide he plunged to endless night."

when the little girl, suiting the action to the
word, dressed in an old velvet coat of her
mother's, and a worsted beard made by the
French maid, plunges, accompanied by the
giggles of her relatives, off the fender stool,
somewhat too obviously pulling up her bard's
gown in front, foremost into the mattress
laid for her.

"Well, it really went off very well," says
Mrs. Mulholland, as the door closes on the
guests, speaking with that air of unaffected
comfort and relief with which we mostly
salute our friends' backs; "and I quite like
Sir Robert!"

"And I like him too, awfully!" cries Sue,
still in her bardish wig and beard, which
have veered a good deal to one side in her
plunge. "He asked me how many prizes
Fezy had taken, and said he was abdominally
small."

They all laugh, but without surprise, for
Sue's malaprops are proverbial.

"Abnormally, Sue."

"Well, abnormally, then; but, Pamela,

did he really come all the way to Anglesey
to see you? Why, he said scarcely anything
to you!"

"That is the joke!" cries Pamela, beginning to skip about and clap her hands.
"He never saw me but once in his life
before, and he did not know me again from
Adam! Poor man! he was very remorseful,
but he did not—that is the joke!"

"I can't say that I see much point in it,"
says Czar dryly, adding: "As I told you,
my dear, he is quite one of our world—a
perfectly presentable person ; but I can't say
that he is well preserved. I am told he is
not much over fifty, but with that 'frosty
pow'"—smiling— "I confess I should have
been inclined to give him ten years more."

"Everybody can't be as young as somebody," replies his wife, giving him a small
fond slap ; and then they all retire. Pamela
follows Anne into her bedroom.

"I will not stay a moment! See, I will
not even put down my candlestick! I know
how you detest back-hair talks ; but"—

putting her arm round her friend's waist, and looking closely into her eyes with the dewy joyousness of her own — "you have enjoyed yourself to-night, haven't you? You did look so bright!"

"Like the sign of the Rising Sun on a pot-house!" replies Anne, half laughing, half grateful, and yet vexed with herself for having worn her heart so openly on her sleeve for even this most friendly daw to peck at.

"You always ludicrously under-rate your own attractiveness; but to-night you must know that you are looking radiant! I know now how you must have looked before you suffered so much; but *how* you must have suffered!"

"I had not a particularly rosy time,' replies Mrs. Bligh, though not expansively, for, indeed, she is of almost as *boutonnée* a nature as Cordelia; "but I dare say no worse than I deserved, and after all" — laughing constrainedly — "you must own that it is better to have one's kicks first and one's halfpence afterwards than *vice-versâ*."

"Halfpence, indeed!" cries Pamela ecstatically. "Thousand-pound notes; and they are only just beginning!"

CHAPTER VIII.

" 'Tis the chief principle to keep your heart
    Under your own obedience ; jest, but love not."

" SUPPOSE that he comes while we are out !"

The suggestion is Pamela's, and is made
on the afternoon of the following day, as the
young Mulhollands and their guests are
gathered about the hall-door, just setting off
on an excursion of the ride and tie kind,
to celebrate Lucile's convalescence. It is
made *sotto voce*, and to one person. That
person shakes her head.

" Not likely ! He was to go to Beaumaris
Church, to choose the site for old Lady
Lascelles' monument."

" He would do that in the morning. That
would leave the afternoon free, and the

Lascelles always bring their people down here. Oh, suppose!"—with an almost tragic emphasis—"just suppose that we find his card when we come back!"

Mrs. Bligh laughs with a gallant air of indifference.

"Why, we will draw lots for it, and whoever gets it shall have it framed and gla——" With a sudden change of tone—"Here he is!"

"The lion has escaped from his cage, and come to frolic with the kids!" says Pamela, making a snatch of congratulation at Anne's nearest hand. "You double-faced woman, you knew it all along!"

And then the sculptor is among them.

"You are going out?" he says, in a tone whose politeness does not quite cover an inflection of disappointment. "My host has gone to a Welsh function. I think he said he was to be made a bard of!"—with a half-smile—"and I— but do not let me delay you. By Jove!"—with an involuntary touch of envy in his voice—"how jolly you all look!"

"Oh, how disappointed Czar will be!" cries little Sue, in a key of heartfelt regret. "He does so love seeing people—seeing anybody."

They all laugh at the *naïveté* of this tribute, and Lucile adds in a shy but civil and "grown-up" voice :

"I'm almost sure that mother is at home. Sue, run and see."

"Mother is setting a Lang Shang hen, and will not thank anybody for disturbing her," says Pamela, arresting by a sudden claw of the shoulder the willing child, who, with her usual eagerness in the pursuit of anyone else's supposed pleasure, is shooting off like an arrow. "Why"—turning to the newcomer with a faintly-deepened colour—"why can't you be content with us? Why can't you come with us?"

She says it with a pretty and happy audacity, which would not have misbeseemed that lovely page who won and flouted Phœbe's rustic heart in the Arden wood; and the person addressed looks back at her with the

pleased gratitude that would naturally be
called forth by the sight of anything so fair,
so amiable, and so sprightly.

"May I really?" he asks eagerly, and,
despite his fifty years, with an accent of young
friskiness in his voice. "I should like it of
all things, but"—with as decided a turning
to Anne as on the previous night—"you
say nothing? Do you endorse the invitation?"

"What a silly question!" is all the answer
she gives—an answer that for once he does
not misread. And then the little *cortége* sets
off. Lucile in a bath-chair, drawn by a
steady pony, which has been substituted,
much to the invalid's annoyance, for the dear
but perilous jackasses; George and Pamela
on either hand; Sue and the dogs skirmishing
on the flanks, and the rear brought up by
the two elders.

On the spirit of the woman, despite the
delightfulness of this arrangement, there rests
a slight cloud. She wishes that it had not
come about through Pamela's management—

wishes it without knowing why, and with the slight but chilling dread superadded that he may think her too obviously assigned to him in the disposition of the little party. He certainly shows no signs of so doing as he steps out actively beside her along the stony upland road with an air of vigorous enjoyment, asking in a voice that keeps that gay holiday touch in it :

"Where are we going? Not that I shall be much wiser when you have told me."

"To Red Wharf Bay."

"So called because the sands are yellow," cries Pamela, with a jolly laugh, throwing the explanation over her shoulder, and giving the fat pony a flick.

The little procession has turned inland, and is crossing a corner of the island, mounting by a rocky road over moorland, between stone walls. Coke has taken off his hat, and with inflated nostrils, parted lips, and dilating eyes, seems imbibing through the channel of every sense the large brightness of the spring sky.

"What light!" he says enviously. "What

might not one do if one had light such as
.this? Is not our want of light in itself enough
to account for the difference between our
work and theirs? I mean the bigwigs in our
line. Could Benvenuto have groped out
his ' Perseus ' in a South Kensington fog ?"

" Then why do not you live in the country ?"

" Why ?" (with a shrug) ; " because I should
cut my throat in a week. Do not look at me so
witheringly " (laughing). " I am like Charles
Lamb ; I love the ' sweet security of streets.' "

" Do you ?" (with an accent of rather pronounced dissent), " I wonder, shall I ever grow
to love the ' sweet security ' of Tite Street ?"

They have reached the highest point of
the rising ground they have been breasting,
and now stop to breathe and look back at
sea and Snowdon hills. A good deal of
snow must have fallen during the night.
What was rain here was evidently snow there.
Carnedd Llewellyn and Carnedd David are
closelier wrapped than they were yestereven.
The clouds are trying different dispositions
of their shadows every moment on crag and

slope, and the light is darting in between and making little meadows of white brightness beside the hard purple lines. All around them as they stand the gorse is blossoming and scenting the fresh air.

"And you would cut your throat if you lived in the country?" says Anne, with an accent of regret at a confession which seems to open such a gulf between them, and a loving look at the smiling Welsh hills. "I dare say you would agree with a friend of mine about mountains. She said she could not bear to live among them; she felt about them as one does when people *will* stand too near one, a desire to push them away, and bid them keep their distance. But then " (reflectively) "she had always lived in a flat country."

"Yes?"

"It was the country I used to live in," her voice involuntarily sinking, and her clear eye darkening, as always when memory approaches her painful past; "there was not a molehill within sight. I used to walk every day along a road as flat as a pancake three

miles out and three miles in. I used to stop
and look over the same gate into the same
field."

" Poor little friend !" (very sympathetically)
"all alone ?"

" How else ? Oh, I did hate that road !
the doctors used to drive me out ; they said
I should break down if they did not. I do
not believe I should. I can see that field
now ; one year it had mangolds, and another
swedes ; and in the winter it was almost
always under water."

" Poor little friend !"

The ejaculation is meant to be fully as compassionately affectionate as on the first occasion ; but Anne's ear seems to detect a flavour
of absence about it, and her eyes, hitherto
averted, snatching a sharp glance at him,
reveal the fact that, with the best intentions
in the world, he is giving her narrative but a
divided attention. The explanation is not
far to seek. The pony-chaise has been drawn
up at about a hundred paces ahead of them,
and Pamela, Sue, and George have taken out

their pocket-knives and cut sprigs and boughs of the lavishly blooming furze. Pamela has stuck a gold spike in the front of her sailor hat. The idea is caught by the others and improved upon. George sticks a second sprig in, then a third, till she has a whole crown of rich gold. Sue must have one too. Then Pamela, invention growing, demands a sprig for each button-hole of her blue home-spun cloak, so does Sue for her dapple-gray; while Lucile, from the chaise, clamours to be equally decked. One makes herself a yellow rosette for each neat shoe; another will not be distanced. Then they dress out the pony, ornamenting headpiece and harness, and shafts; and then—sufficient reason for the sculptor's abstraction —Pamela comes flying with her pretty pricked fingers full of odorous yellow tributes to decorate her friend too. But the friend will have none of them; and says so, with a trenchantness which brings up a little cloud of disappointed surprise over the radiant carnation of the girl's cheek, and causes Coke to strike in with a hasty playful appeal, in which Anne's jealous ear seems to detect a rebuke to herself.

"Am I to be kept out? I, who love finery? Make me as fine as you can," holding out hat and coat lapel.

He will not be content till, as in the case of her own cloak, every button-hole has its flaming glory. An exclamation from the direction of the pony-chaise alone brings the toilette to an end. The large gorse branch, which has been stuck in over the pony's forehead, naturally is not long in pricking its ears, and with a shake of its head off it starts. George grabs at the reins, which have been chucked carelessly on its back, wo-a-ing lustily to it to stop, and the others, reinforced by Miss Capel-Smith, and, alas! by the sculptor, shouting with happy fun, scamper after. The runaway, being much too fat and mature in years to enjoy violent exercise for its own sake, is soon brought to a standstill; but by this time they are all in such a fine flow of spirits that they wish for a repetition of the race; Pamela gets into the chair with Lucile, though there is really only room for one. Sue snatches the reins out of George's hand, and mischievously "tcl-ing" up the pony, away they go down a steep pitch, galloping and screaming ; half frightened, half delighted, over jolting new-laid stones, over the wayside grass ; one side of the Bath-chair up, the other down ; hovering over the edge of a ditch, nearly in it ; rescued by a timely jerk of the reins on the brink. At the bottom of the hill they stop —at least they try to do so ; but the impetus given them by their rush carries them half-way up the next incline before they can really pull up.

They are at a standstill at last, and exchanging inquiries, ejaculations, and reproaches, breathless and almost unintelligible from laughter. The sculptor is the first to regain his gravity, and with a half-shamefaced look goes to meet his late companion, who, alone uninfected by the frenzied frolicsome-ness, and yet reproaching herself for not having caught it, is soberly descending the steep pitch which the Bacchic rout had but now rolled and tumbled down in such childish glee.

" No wonder you are curling your lip at us !" says Coke, half deprecatingly, and yet still with that frisky ring in his voice.

" Indeed, I am doing nothing of the kind ! I know that boys will be boys."

It is meant for a jest, which indeed it is. Nor is he at all less conscious than she that he came of age the year she was born. But no man of fifty, however little he may play at youth, enjoys a fleer, even a sportive one, at his age. A sort of annoyed blush skims over his mobile face as he answers, without ill-humour, but also without the holiday tone of his former sentence :

" That is a very just rebuke !"

" It is not a rebuke !" cries she eagerly, too late repenting of her waspish pleasantry. " It is a plain statement of fact : in myself I am years older than you. I never had the chance of being young when I was young, and now it is too old to begin."

He has resumed his place at her side, and has dropped into a pace as staid as hers, while the rest of the *cortége* gets into motion again, and moves on demurely now ahead of them.

" If you had had my life," she goes on in a key of almost pathetic appeal, as he answers her paradoxical assertion only by a gentle head-shake, "you would wonder that I am not even more morose and fractious than I am."

" When you took those dreary walks, and looked over that gate at the mangolds !"

She feels that this careful repetition of her words is to prove to her how well he had listened.

" Yes."

" And you were quite alone ? Had not even a dog ?"

" Not even a dog ; it was out of the question for me to have a dog. He could not have borne its barking."

" And that went on for—how long ?"

The pause before the two last words

implies a reluctant admission that he has forgotten the extent of her probation, though both are alike aware that it is not the first time she has confided it to him.

"Eight years!"

"Eight years!" his mind wandering back over the corresponding period of his own life —years of engrossing work, growing fame, swelling fortune.

"One would have thought that in such a life I might at least have cultivated my mind, have absorbed a good deal out of books; but even that was quite out of the question. I never could count upon an unbroken quarter of an hour. Whenever I was not in his room I was listening for his bell. For eight years I was listening for a bell! And yet when the end came, when I need never listen again, oh how dreary I felt! Nobody would believe I was sorry. I gave up trying to persuade them. I could not help laughing over my letters of condolence, they read so much more like congratulation," after a moments pause. "I never could persuade

even him ; he often said, ' You poor soul,
how pleased you will be when I am dead !'
and at last I only answered, ' Yes, shall
not I ?"

"And when ? how long ago ?"—his sympathy genuine and lively, but his memory
again a little at fault.

' Two years, but that first year does not
count. I cannot remember how it passed.
I think I must have been dead too, and then
I came to life again, and then I went abroad,
and then I took a house in Tite Street, and
then "—her tone lightening, and her face
breaking into smiles—" I met a lion in a
Dorsetshire snowstorm. You see," between
jest and earnest, "you have been the cul-
minating point of my life's history."

" What should I have done without you in
that snowstorm ?" In another key, " That
absurd girl ! what a madcap she is ! She
will never be satisfied till she has them all in
the ditch."

He quickens his pace as he speaks, and
comes up again with the Bath-chair, round

the brow of whose patient steed Miss Pamela
is again arranging her aureole of painful gold,
in the obvious hope of pricking him up into
a second spurt of artificial liveliness. It is
only with great difficulty, and after a lively
wrangle, that she is dissuaded. That wrangle,
during which Mrs. Bligh, standing a little
apart, looks at the view, combined with their
previous dawdling, has made them so late
that they never get to their proposed destination after all. They turn back before they
reach the bay, which they see and hear
creaming and gently singing with its
sheltered succession of crescent - shaped
billowlets below them, in the sunlight. Now
and then a pompously threatening dark rain-
cloud sails up and shakes out three sprayey
drops from its skirts upon them ; but it is
quickly driven off seawards, before it can
even damp them.

They return in a different order from that
in which they came, though that is not the
fault of the sculptor, who would be well
content to drop behind again with his ally,

and, while his artist eye is pleased by the
graceful antics of the young girls ahead of
him, reward Mrs. Bligh's confidence by that
intimate talk about himself and his work,
which to a man of his stamp, and in the case
of a thoroughly trusted and warmly-liked
woman, is such a genuine enjoyment. But
Anne keeps so persistent a hold of one side
of the Bath-chair, and talks with such a
frenzy of determination to its inmate, that
after one or two oblique efforts to induce her
to detach her grip, he desists. He does his
best even then, by making a pendant to her
on the other side, and shooting remarks at
her across the convalescent. But it is not
the same thing as on the outward journey ;
and once again he feels that sense of chill
and repulse which her unaccountable snub-
bings and shortnesses have before inspired
him with.

And yet he must have thought the excursion a success, for next day, when they
repeat it, he is again one of them. It is
unlikely that Sir Thomas Lascelles is a

second time to be made a bard, but yet his
guest again manages to elude his hospitality;
on what pretext they none of them—since
all are glad to have him—too curiously in-
quire. They go to Penmaen to-day to see
a ruined priory, and a lighthouse beyond it;
and either because they have more fixity of
purpose, or the weather—it is a colourless
uniform day, like a dull man's mind—holds
out less temptation to loiter, they do really
arrive at their promised point in this case.
Unlike yesterday, their road runs at first
sheltered between hedges, high hedges,
where the new brown buds of the quickset
hedge show against patches of monotonous
evergreen, then out on an exposed and sea-
washed tract of sedgy land, over which the
tide must once have rolled, and where now
the gorse lights its yellow fires; up to Penmaen, where a painfully newly restored
church, with fresh pointed bricks, contrasts
the graceful decay of the ruined walls of the
ancient monastery, in whose roofless en-
closures chickens stroll, and along whose

face an enormously old ivy tree stretches like an apricot on a garden wall. Up a steep pitch, over a blowy hill, whose fine grass is nibbled down by rabbits, of which this green slope is a warren, down, down to where the black and white lighthouse stands, now at low tide scarcely touched by the surf, which at flow foams so high around it. In the watches of the past night, Anne has taken herself seriously to task for her conduct during the Red Wharf Bay excursion ; for her stupid and surly want of confidence in her friend and his liking ; for her lack of spring and of sympathetic gaiety. To her pillow she has made many a penitent vow, that if fate gives her another chance, she will be more cheerful, more skittish, more in tune with her surroundings. A playfulness, *de commande*, is not as a rule worth much ; but hers is happily not put to a very severe test, as on this second trip the level of spirits of the whole party is distinctly less boisterously high than on the former one.

Pamela, who both times has given the

keynote, is for some reason in a soberer vein,
and walks along so steadily and with a
demureness so gentle—gentle even to the
discarded George—that the latter is em-
boldened to offer her timidly a little rabbit's
skull, bleached and bare, which he has picked
up, and of which he surreptitiously keeps
back the lower jaw : and when the odd present is carelessly accepted, half furtively
hides his portion in his pocket. The elders,
following in the rear, witness the little
transaction.

"That is the oddest love-token I ever saw,"
says Coke, laughing. "He had better have
given it to Fezy ; he would have appreciated
it more."

"Would he?" with interest. "There! I
told you! She has dropped it already. Why
do you pick it up?" (as he stoops to retrieve
the castaway love-gift).

"Why? I do not know; I suppose because I never can help a sneaking tenderness towards anything or anybody that is
dropped."

"You certainly ought to have a tenderness for young Mulholland, then, since there is no doubt as to her having dropped him."

"Has she? Well, I know it is inconsistent, but I am glad of that."

"Why?" (a little breathlessly).

"Why! Oh, because" (indifferently), "if people must be mated—I do not myself see any necessity—but if they must, I think it is as well that they should not be mismated. I never can quite pardon Shakespeare for having given Celia to Oliver, or Hero to that sweep Claudio!"

"I expect that a good many of Shakespeare's couples were not very happy in their married life," replies Mrs. Bligh thoughtfully. "I am not very sure about even Benedick and Beatrice; Oliver, of course, beat Celia. I am afraid that Angelo and Mariana led but a cat-and-dog life; and I must say I hope that Bertram paid out Helena for having entrapped him. I never could bear Helena."

"No? and yet she is the mouthpiece for

some of the sweetest sayings about love that Shakespeare ever uttered. Ah, here we are! How would you like to live in a lighthouse, madam ?"

" George has gone for the key," cries Sue, sending her childish voice down the sea wind to them. " We are all to go inside, and the man is to show us the resolving light."

" Of course you need not come," says Pamela, approaching her friend, the red light in her eyes as bright with expectation as Sue's " resolving" one can be. " That is if you had rather not ; nor you either," waving a little larch wand, lately cut by George out of a hedge for her, in the direction of Coke, to show that she means him.

" Of course I shall come," replies Anne stoutly, with a hurried recollection of her midnight resolve to be not outdone in youth or enterprise, even by Sue or Fezy. " How easy it looks—only those three little steps !"

But the three little steps, like many other things in life, wear a very different aspect when looked at close, from that which they

present when seen from a distance. The
lighthouse is reached now at low tide by a
path made of three narrow planks laid abreast,
and furnished with an iron handrail; and
when this is passed, and the base of the
structure reached, Mrs. Bligh perceives how
razor-edged, how slippery, how strait, the
steps which from the hill had looked as easy
of ascent as the *perron* of a Georgian country-
house really are. Her heart fails her, and
despite Sue's earnest adjuration and handsome offer, "Oh, do come, I will push you
from behind very hard; and then if you fall
I shall be killed too!" she lets the young
ones—though with a slight heart-pinch at
the thought of her own oldness and want of
agility—go without her. Coke stays beside
her—at least, he really meant to do so; and
together they amusedly watch the little girl
crawling up first, holding tight on to the rail
on each side, while her closely following
brother restrains her lively petticoats from
indulging a lively impulse to fly over her
head. She has reached the top in safety,

and now it is Pamela's turn. She is generally daring and hardy enough, but now she hesitates.

"If you hold me down as tightly as you did Sue," she says, eyeing her expectant squire with unveiled distrust, "I shall not be able to move my legs at all!"

"I seem never to be able to do anything right of late," he answers affronted, and, turning on his heel, begins to retrace his steps across the slippery planks to where the Bath-chair and Lucile are waiting on the hillside.

Pamela on her part makes a feint of attempting the ascent unaided. But it is so evident a one, and the young man's lagging retreat partakes so obviously of the same character, that it is apparent to the meanest understanding that necessity on one side and tenderness on the other will, if they are left to themselves, soon effect a *rapprochement* between the couple. There is not the smallest need for anyone else to interfere, and yet Mrs. Bligh does so. The sculptor is leaning over the rails, his attention strayed away from the squabbling youth and maiden, listening pleased to the sea-song, and looking at the rocklets below him, all covered with the little bladders of the coarse yellow-brown sea-tang, and the much more delicate briny weeds that live in the mimic pools and hollows left by the tide. He is fancifully likening them to land things : the pink ones to sea-heather, the green to meadow grass, when his friend's voice breaks into his reverie :

" Ought not you to go to the rescue ?"

She makes the suggestion : firstly, because she has a perfectly groundless suspicion that he wishes it ; and secondly, because she herself had very much rather that he did not.

" The rescue !" he answers, with a quite genuine slight start. " Whose rescue ? Oh, I see ! By all means."

Two minutes later Pamela, flushed and with wind-loosened hair, is blowing kisses to Anne from the lighthouse doorway, up to which she has been skilfully, swiftly. and lightly piloted, and then with her guide disappears in the interior. Mrs. Bligh rests her arms on the rails as nearly as possible in the same spot as that lately occupied by Coke, tries to look at exactly the same seaweeds, and to catch the train of thought they had suggested to him. As she does so, an undisguisedly angry voice sounds in her ear : " I see you are my enemy still." She does not answer young Mulholland, but to her own heart she says, " Not nearly so much as my own."

CHAPTER IX.

THE Mulholland family no longer make company of Anne, as is apparent by the freedom with which, on the evening following the Penmaen trip, they are pursuing their usual course of every-day occupation and rough family jokes. The only exception is the head, who is trying to read his *Morning Post* without glasses by holding the paper at an immense distance from his eyes, and has just snubbed the objectionable librarian for an officious offer to seek his spectacle-case for him ; but, like most under-bred persons, this one is quite unsnubbable, and only follows up his proposal by a jocose anecdote of some other elderly gentleman who was supposed to

have said, "My sight is as good as ever; I
only want my arm lengthened."

It is received with a frozen silence, but its
author goes on chuckling over it for several
minutes. Lucile in the tearing spirits of
young convalescence and Sue are having a
quite noisy scuffle, which neither of their
parents appears to hear, and the object of
which is on Lucile's part the snatching away
and on Sue's the retention of a half-written
letter addressed by the latter to a correspondent, and which the elder sister is mischievously anxious to read aloud for the diversion
of the company. The war, rendered unequal
by the fact that Lucile is still supported by a
stick, is being waged with uncertain fortune
until George decides its issue by unexpectedly
filching the contested document out of the
hands of both combatants, and reading it out
in a loud, level voice over their heads.

"There are two very curious bridges here,
one is a suspention bridge, the other is a
tubibular bridge, because it resembles a
gigantic tobe."

The little scribe's family burst into a roar of laughter, while she herself hovers between giggles and tears, crying :

" Oh, Czar, you too! you *are* unkind !"

" I am sure you do not mean that, Sue !" strikes in the librarian perkily. " I know that you think your pappy a dear, kind old gentleman !"

In a second everybody stops laughing.

"You are looking pale, Nan !" says the hostess ; " we must not let these young lunatics tear you to pieces ; they forget that you are not quite the same age as themselves !"

This imputation on her juvenility leaves its object calm, but her young disciple reddens with indignation.

" If people are all young together, I do not see that a year or two makes much difference. I am sure we were all one as young as another to-day."

" Including our poor Coke ?" suggests Czar with a sneer.

" Yes, including ' our poor Coke ' " (sturdily) ; "of course that is a joke, he is not young, and he does not pretend to be ; but Anne *is* young !"

"Of course she is ! Your birthday is the 20th of February, Nan, is not it ? I remember it because it came between Constance Fletcher's and Laura Wilde's. I have quite lost sight of Constance, and someone told me that Laura had gone to the bad. I hope it is not true."

She expresses this hope with an air of such absolute snug indifference that Mrs. Bligh smiles, but does not answer, because her attention is at this moment claimed by the sight of Fezy, whom she now sees standing on the hearthrug shaking her lace pocket-handkerchief like a rat. He has stolen it out of her pocket so softly that she has not till now become aware of her loss.

"*Isn't* he clever ?" cries his little owner ecstatically ; "he always goes to the right side because he knows that people have their pockets on the right side. Oh, I *do* hope he has not done it much harm !"

This unlikely aspiration is so far from being realized that Mrs. Bligh's sole course is good-naturedly to reassure the little girl by telling her that it is only her second-best pocket-handkerchief, and to make over the wreck to George, who, anxious to display in turn the accomplishments of his own favourite, makes it up into an improbable mouse and throws it to the end of the long room for Jim the terrier to pursue and worry, which he does with such artistic thoroughness as to throw poor Fezy's talents into the shade. Conscious of this, mad with mortification and envy, yet too cowardly to dispute the prize, the tiny performer lies eclipsed in an arm-chair, easing his feelings by a short angry bark each time that the small damp ball and the scampering terrier's feet slither together over the parquet.

"It is very good-natured of you to pretend that you like their harum-scarum expeditions," says Mrs. Mulholland, taking advantage of a war of words which has arisen between the dog-owners, and in which Pamela has been called in as umpire; " but, of course, I know that it is only good-nature, and so I told Lady Lascelles to-day, when she came to arrange about the visit to the Quarries for Monday; she made rather a point of having you, but I really do not see why, when you have come here to enjoy yourself, you should be made use of to entertain other people's guests."

If there is any gratification to be derived from this speech by the person to whom it is addressed, it lies in the evidence it affords of how very much better she must have disguised her sentiments than is usually possible to her. But her satisfaction, such as it is, does not hinder her saying resolutely, though with a laugh :

" I am afraid I do not often do anything out of good-nature; I should like to go on Monday. I have never seen a slate-quarry."

" There is not much to see "— disparagingly - " and you have to be dragged up cliffs as steep as the side of a house in little open trucks ; I can't think how any head can stand it. I am sure you would be much happier at home with Czar and me."

"Pray do not include *me !*" cries he huffily; "upon my word, our friend Coke, for a man who is supposed to have come down here professionally, is taking it pretty coolly; here to-day, there to-morrow. I fail to see where the business comes in."

" He has spent the whole of each morning in making sketches and taking measurements for the monument in the church," says Anne, picking up the cudgels for her absent friend, and calling herself a fool for doing so ; "and apparently Sir Thomas is satisfied with him, as he now wishes him to do also a bust of Lady Lascelles."

" H'm ! I wonder how many more effigies of herself that dear little lady will have before she is content !"

"A bust of Lady Lascelles !" cries his wife in a tone of lively interest. " I wonder she never mentioned it when she was here to-day ! I dare say she was afraid of your chaffing her; you know you are a little satirical sometimes to her, though she *is* a great favourite. Oh, Czar "—with a sudden inspiration—" how I wish that *you* would sit to him! Have you any idea "—to Anne— " what his charge is? and would he make a reduction in the case of a particularly good subject ?"

" I have not an idea," with an inward smile, given to the recollection of Coke's delighted comparison of his host's face to that of old Nellie, the ourang-outang. " I believe—I imagine—that his price would be about £500!"

" £500!"—this from Czar—" do you mean to say that he has the conscience to ask £500 for a mere bust, just head and shoulders? I like his effrontery! Why, Marochetti himself——"

But what Marochetti himself either did, or did not, will never now be certainly known, for at this juncture there arises a hideous clamour of dogs and men. It springs from the fact that at one last supernatural bound of the pocket-handkerchief mouse, and capture of it by Jim, Fezy loses all self-control, and, casting prudence to the winds, leaps from his armchair, and flies at the terrier. The latter unhesitatingly retorts by a very sincere nip into the beautiful black *jabot* under his little chin ; while Lassie—always a rather underhand character—seeing here a good opportunity of paying off old scores, plants her teeth in the happily thick silk of his nape. All their owners at once hurl themselves into the fray, and amid a mingled din of howls, growls, tears, and smacks, the evening ends.

When Monday comes it is apparent that the energy of Mrs. Bligh's assertion of her wish to visit the slate-quarries has been of service to her, since no more efforts at dissuasion are made. She sets off accompanied by reiterated hopes from her host that she may enjoy herself, uttered in a tone which plainly shows how assured he is that she will not. His family leave him, making ostentatious and unnecessary—since he had not been invited—actions of thanksgiving that he is not of the party. The third of any series ought always to be the best; and surely this third and crowning excursion, exceeding the previous ones so far in scope and ambition, must exceed them proportionately in enjoyment too. It opens auspiciously. Sir Thomas drives his own coach, but in thoughtful deference to a dislike, carelessly expressed on a previous day by Anne for that form of conveyance, a victoria has been provided for her; and in that victoria it is soon clear that the sculptor is meant to be her companion. She fancies that he looks surprised at the arrangement, and at once asks him in her shortest voice whether he would not rather go on the coach. He answers her—as how can he help doing?— and with every appearance of veracity, that he had rather not, and seats himself beside her with an expression of complete, if not ecstatic, content.

"Now we are going to enjoy ourselves," he says in a tone of easy playfulness, that yet to her ears conveys a very gentle admonishment. "We are going to stroke each other's fur the right way the whole day, and not say anything that is not perfectly pleasant to one another, for who knows when we shall have the chance of another ride together in a one-horse shay? Are you agreed?"

"Do you wish me to commit perjury?" she asks; but her voice is no longer short, and she smiles.

It is an uncertain blowy day: now brilliant, now sulky; the sea, a mere dark sheet a moment ago, suddenly covered all over with silver scales. By the side of the charming Straits they pass, across the noble Menai Bridge, since the quarries lie in Carnarvonshire. Coke is obviously inclined to be silent, and, despite his announcement of a determination to enjoy himself, apparently somewhat out of spirits. His companion's anxious desire to discover the cause shapes itself by-and-by into the query:

"You are really going back to London to-night?"

"Yes; I shall catch the night mail at Chester."

"You are glad to go?"

"To any other woman I should, of course, say 'No'; but to my conscience"—with a look of affectionate confidence—"I may indulge myself in the luxury of speaking truth. I *am* glad. I can't work with comfort anywhere but in my studio. I can't sleep in a strange bed. I miss my violent ride in the park in the morning. I suppose"—with a smile—"that I am like an old watch, which after a good shaking goes again!"

Until the candour of this answer disabuses her, Mrs. Bligh had not realized how much of hope had lurked in her mind that the sculptor's depression owed its cause to the ending of his rural holiday.

"You have not seen my new horse," he pursues—a livelier tone already evident in his voice at the thought of his departure— "he is the colour of a donkey. I think there must have been a mésalliance in his family! I saw him in the street one day being trotted out for someone, and he turned his head and looked at me as if he said, ' I wish you would buy me '; so I got the vet. to find out who he belonged to, and outbid the fellow he did not like, and now we are great friends. I must ride him round to Tite Street some day to show him to you ; but "— with impatience— " you will not be there !"

" No."

" When *are* you coming back ?" with friendly urgency.

She shakes her head doubtfully.

" I have not very much to come back to. I shall not find a Rayon d'Or and six dead brewers, and an equestrian general, waiting for me on my hearthrug."

" But if you like, you may find the guilty author of them all there," replies he, laughing. Then more seriously, " Without any joke, I wish you would come home soon. You may think I do not mean it— that it is only *'Blague'* ; but I assure you the knowledge that there is a tribunal in a little house in Tite Street, before which I must appear, has more than once made me refuse work, which otherwise I should probably for the sake of filthy lucre "—with a shrug—"have accepted."

"I wonder is that true?" she asks doubt-fully, her eyes averted from him, and resting on the stone wall, which—hideous but philan-thropic, built to employ workmen in a famine year—girdles for seven miles the park of the owner of the Llanberis Quarries.

"Why is it that I never can get you to realize what a boon a *genuine* friendship with a woman is to a man?" Her ear detects very readily the slight accent on the adjec-tive. "The relations between men and women are so apt to be spoilt by the intro-duction of a—a spurious element, that I do not know "—with gentle reproach—"why one should be suspected of lying when one rejoices at having secured the real thing."

It is dull of her not to have any answer ready, not even a sign of acquiescence.

"Was not it "—he goes on, and there is a slight indication of discomfort in his voice at her silence—" Balzac who said : 'Ce qui rend les amitiés indissolubles, et double leur charme est un sentiment qui manque à l'amour, la certitude.' I wish "—kindly—" I could put a little of that *certitude* into you ; you would then be an ideal friend !"

The coach ahead of them has stopped ; the little mining village, which is the *point de départ* of their climb, being reached. An hour later they are being wound up the side of a cliff, on an incline of a gradient not much less steep than the side of a house, in little trucks, each with a backless board thrown across it as sole seat.

" It is *so* delightful !" Sue has explained as they set off. " You feel as if you must fall backwards. Mother shut her eyes and screamed the whole way. I wonder will you ?"

But Mrs. Bligh does not. Her head is a strong one, and to her the bird-like feeling of triumphantly mounting brings into it nothing but elation, as she looks down on the slate rocks ; on the profound Llanberis lake, which is yearly being diminished by the heaps of refuse slate weekly and monthly advancing their feet further and further into its waters; on the men like little flies walking about below. And then they are slung up into the heart of the quarries themselves, and find what a grand meaning there lies in that word —which to most of us calls up only memories of the tearful essays in arithmetic of our childhood—the homely word "slate." Here, they stand surrounded by sheer walls of it; purple and lilac, and green and olive; not a scrap of vegetation anywhere; sheer walls and peaks and precipices of the sombre, yet many-coloured splendour. One above another rise the galleries where the quarrymen are working, some of the dark tunnel-mouths now high up in air showing to what a depth the cliff has been blasted and pickaxed away since those tunnels were bored. There is something of awful in the thought of the way in which man—in some aspects so puny and ephemeral an insect—is changing the face of what we were wont to call the everlasting hills!

Everlasting, indeed! Whither has disappeared the mountain block which once
filled the huge gap now yawning between
yon two parted promontories? Within the
last few months it has been blown bodily
away ; the great rock dissolved, as it were,
into thin air. Soon, probably, the yet en-
during crags will have melted away with all
the noble tints and shades on their riven sides,
before the might and the malice of their tiny,
evanescent, yet all-powerful foe.

Anne has sat down to rest on a green gray
ledge in a part of the quarry which has
assumed the air of a gigantic amphitheatre ;
range above range of semicircular seats, on
which Titans, or yet huger than Titans,
might sit to look on at some giant fight or
game or race, in the arena below. On the
lake's further side, cloud-capped Snowdon
and his vassal hills seem looking on with fear
and dread at the havoc wrought on their
brethren opposite.

Mrs. Bligh is for the moment alone, the
party having drifted in different directions.

Sue has carried off some of them to a shed where men are at work splitting the slates, which requires nicety, and cutting them into shape; while Pamela, clinging to George's hand to preserve her balance with a tenacity which nothing but the instinct of self-preservation could give, is craning over a sheer rock-edge to watch a slate-loaded iron basket worked by a crane slowly mount the scarped hillside.

"What a strange idea of pleasure!"

The widow starts. She had not imagined the sculptor to be near her; nor that his eyes, like her own, were watching Miss Capel - Smith's rather perilous gymnastics. They have not exchanged words since their *tête-à-tête* drive, which has left a vague impression of dissatisfaction on both their minds. "It will be very perverse of her" laughing—"if she insists on breaking her neck before I have succeeded in getting her to sit for me."

"Is she going to sit for you?" rather quickly.

" That is more than I can say ; I cannot get a rational answer out of her. I can't induce her to believe that I mean it seriously."

" No ?"

" I can't get either ' Yes ' or ' No ' out of her ; and when I thought I had driven her into a corner, she escaped me by murmuring something about her parents.   I wish nobody had parents.   I wish every woman was born a widow.   Do you suppose it is true, and that her parents would object ?"

" Since you wish to represent her as a Nereid " — drily — " I think it is not un-likely."

" I do not see "—warmly—" what harm it could do either them or her to lend me her pretty little head ; and whether I call her Ligea or Cassiopæia or St. Cecilia, is surely my affair—not theirs."

" Didn't I ?"—still drily—" understand you to say that you wished to have her dear little hands, too, to twist in your seahorse's mane ?"

"Well, it would not do her much harm to lend me them too, but, as it happens, I do not want them. I have been looking at them, and there is not much character in them — there seldom is in young girls' hands."

They are both silent for a minute or two, watching the subject of their conversation, who has by this time recovered her equilibrium, and repudiated the support (which even from here they can see to be offered with such nervous eagerness) of young Mulholland. Anne is the first to speak, but her utterance, when it comes, sounds rather enigmatical, and is not elucidated by her eyes, which are fastened on the dark Lynn.

" I should have thought that your simplest plan would have been to secure a permanent sitter."

" A permanent sitter? How do you mean?"

" One who could never expose you to the mortification of a refusal ; whose duty it would be to pose whenever and for whatever you choose."

"Do you mean a professional model? But, of course, I have half a dozen."

"I do not mean a professional model." She pauses, and then goes on in a constrained voice, and with averted eyes : "To most professional men a wife is a costly luxury ; to an artist she is a prime economy, and a first-class investment."

"A wife!" he repeats, in a tone of surprised consternation, which, had she been open at the moment to impressions of the ludicrous, must have made her laugh. "Is that what your mysterious innuendoes have been driving at? *Et tu, Brute!* Well, I did not expect it of you. I thought that you, at least, were above the vulgar error of believing every man must have an omnivorous wish to marry every woman he looks or does not look at."

Coke speaks with a not unnatural irritation, and with the speed of one anxious to close an unwelcome theme.

"Vulgar I may be, and no doubt am!"
retorts she, highly nettled, and wilfully mis-
understanding ; "but I still think that when
a man is perpetually devouring a girl with
his eyes, it is a not unnatural inference that
he wishes to appropriate her."

No sooner is this extremely objectionable
sentence out of her mouth than she bitterly
regrets its utterance, but, like most repen-
tances, hers comes too late.

He looks silently at her with a half-in-
credulous displeasure, and moves away to
meet Sue, who is coming flying towards
them.

"We are to go back in the workmen's
train!" cries she, breathless with excitement ;
"and Sir Thomas has asked Mr. ——"—
the agent, and a personal friend of the
Lascelles—"to let as many of us as there
is room for travel on the engine. Oh, I
hope there will be room for *me!*"

"You shall go instead of me—I will give
you up my place," replies the sculptor good-
naturedly, in a voice which bears no trace

of the late ruffling of his temper; and taking Sue by the hand he walks off with her to make the proposed sacrifice.

The workmen's train carries the quarry-men back to Port Dinorwic after work-hours, and on its engine, worked by Mr. ——— himself, Mrs. Bligh and the enraptured Sue make their descent. In the interest of observing the 1,200 quarrymen sitting to-gether close as sardines on the loaded slate-trucks, and in the excitement of watching how many of the 2,400 pendant fustian legs are grazed by the perilously close rock wall as the train bends round an abrupt curve, the little girl is so absorbed that the grown woman may enjoy her own reflections un-disturbed. At Port Dinorwic Coke is to quit the party, in order to pursue his journey to London.

Must they part thus? At first it seems that it will be so. It appears obvious to her that in the last rapidly-fleeting moments, while the horses are being put to, he pointedly avoids her. She cannot let him go without any apology or peacemaking overture. He is already drawing on his gloves, and has said his last graceful civilities to Lady Lascelles, when, in desperation, she walks without any subterfuge straight up to him.

"It was a temptation of the devil," she says, in a low key: "are you very, very angry with me?"

Her voice shakes perceptibly, and there is an evident sincerity in her eyes.

He looks back at her, softened, but still jarred.

"I am never angry with you," he answers, taking her hand in farewell; "but when you say those sort of things, dear friend, you rub a little of the bloom off our friendship."

CHAPTER X.

"I AM the last person in the world to deny what a boon to us the Lascelles are," says Mrs. Mulholland the next morning at breakfast.

"You might as well deny that two and two make four, as that they head our rather scanty list of blessings," interrupts her husband peevishly.

"I do not deny it, but"—with good-humoured pertinacity—"what I do maintain is that they are unsettling. One can't fix one's mind to anything when one never knows at what hour of the morning Lady Lascelles may spring a serene highness, or an ambassador, or a sculptor, through the garden door upon one."

"As many serene highnesses and ambassa-
dors as she pleases; I am not much afraid
of lacking subjects of conversation with
them, and introduced by whatever door it
may please her whimsical little ladyship;
but as to her last *protégé*, I tell her fairly
I am inclined to pick a quarrel with
her!"

"Do not set her against the poor man!"
—compassionately—"I dare say he is very
good in his own line; and, indeed, he must
be, if he asks the prices Nan told us. Now,
Nan, I appeal to you"—rising from the
table, since the meal is ended, and putting
her hand on her schoolfellow's shoulder, as
they pass into the drawing-room—"shall not
we be much more cosy to-day, having ourselves to ourselves? I do not feel as if I
had had the least bit of good of you yet. I
do not grudge you to Czar, but I do grudge
you to perfect strangers. I have not heard
a single word about your life since we parted,
except, of course, just the main facts of your
marriage, and the —— in fact"—doubtfully

—" I never feel quite sure whether you like talking about it."

" I had rather talk about yours."

"Ah, you poor dear thing! it must seem wonderfully bright to you; but"—reassuringly —" I have one little shoe-pinch too."

" Have you?　I am sorry to hear it."

" Not a very uncommon one—only L. S. D. I could do with a little more money—not for myself, of course ; when one has the main thing of life, one does not much mind about the extras—but for Czar."

" You look so well off."

"You mean that we have carriages and horses, and plenty of servants?　Ah, that is his royal sort of way!　Once I proposed to him to reduce the establishment—send away one of the footmen, and a housemaid or two—and have fewer in the kitchen ; and he made no objection, not a word ; but he went about looking so drooping, so utterly wretched, that, of course, I never had the heart to repeat the suggestion."

" No ?"

"Then, naturally, he would like to do more for George. He—George—has never been to either University, because his father could not afford to send him—literally could not afford—that is, unless he gave up his own rooms in St. James's Place, and his little summer trips to Dieppe, and, in fact, everything that makes life life to him! He told the boy so himself, with tears in his eyes; that is why his children adore him so. He treats them like friends and equals. George was so touched!"

"Was he? Poor George!"

"Then, Lucile—you see what a really remarkable turn she has for animal-drawing? He longs to give her a chance. Indeed, one day I found her crying, because he had just told her that he meant to put down his Whitechapel, in order to be able to give her some really good lessons! Of course, none of us would hear of such a sacrifice, but those are the generous kind of impulses that he has!"

An hour later, Mrs. Bligh and Pamela

are walking through the crisp March morning towards the noble old feudal castle of Beaumaris, which stands, with the little town that has grown up at its feet, close beside the Straits, across which the Snowdon Range has looked down upon it for its 500 years of stout life and robust decay. It is girdled by a high loopholed wall, bursting out at intervals into round towers.

They go inside and pace the grassy circle —once, perhaps, a moat—between the outer and the inner walls, and enter, through a broken arch, the turfy square, where the donjon fronts them, and where the still massive though ruinous windows darken like eye-sockets in the keep's gray face. They sit down to rest on a bench, and after a minute or two of silence Pamela says :

"Why is it that, as often as one is particularly comfortable, one is sure to feel Fate giving one a push from behind, and telling one to move on ?"

"Does one? I do not see the present application."

"No? But of course not! Why should you? It is only that I am feeling just that push at the present moment; I should like" —with girlish exaggeration—"to stay here with you for ever, and I know that if I did right I should go back to London to-morrow."

"Why?"—quickly—"have you——"

She stops, unable to put into words the senseless fear that assails her as to the motive that may dictate the girl's proposed return.

"Have I—what?" asks Pamela, looking up, puzzled by something in her companion's voice. "No, I have not—anything"—laughing—"but I know that if I had any sense of honour—sometimes I think I have not—I should be off from here by that horrible jangling station 'bus to Bangor to-morrow morning. I see by unerring signs that a crisis is approaching."

"Really?" replies Anne, genuinely interested, and with an inward blush at the thought of how entirely her absorption in

her own concerns has blinded her to everything outside them. "What reason have
you for thinking so?"

"Have not you noticed"—again laughing,
but with vexation—"with what touching
iteration poor dear Mrs. Mulholland keeps
telling me that I am one of the family?"

"Ye—es"—not quite truthfully, but
ashamed to acknowledge her own want of
observation—"I think I have."

"And Czar has quite given up trying to
kiss me on the stairs!"

"That at least is clear gain."

"Even he"—pursues Pamela, with a
short smile—"sees the impossibility of
making love to his own daughter-in-law."

"I should think so!"—emphatically.

"But I am not so much the gainer as
you suppose"—gloomily—"I do not find
the stairs any safer. I have only exchanged
the father for the son."

"Does George pounce out upon you too?"

"Oh no, poor fellow! there is no pouncing
about it. Only he is always on the landing,

or at the foot of the staircase, looking reproachful, and begging me to tell him what he has done, and why I am so changed. Of course, I can't explain to him that growth is not change."

Anne is silent. Her companion's assertion, made once before, as to having outgrown her old lover in intellectual stature, always gives her a sense of discomfort and guilt. Her eye rests absently on the tercentenary ivy which hangs on the wall, still and unreached by the March wind that is loudly singing and shouting to the white horses in the Straits outside, like a charioteer that is urging those foaming steeds to higher speed.

" He is so under-educated!"—continues the girl irritably, boxing a daisy's ears with her umbrella point—"so limited ; his horizon is no further from his nose than that!" indicating a space not wider than an inch from her own disdainful feature.

" Poor fellow! That is more his misfortune than his fault."

"Yes; I know he has only to thank that abominable old Czar, who sent him to a cheap and nasty school, for fear of having to buy less expensive wigs and teeth, and have fewer of the 'parties fines' he is always talking of at Bignon's, if he put him to a decent one; but the fact remains all the same"—with a resolute shake of the head —"he is as narrow as *that!*" indicating another minute space with her finger and thumb. "If you begin to talk to him about anything—art, literature—you are pulled up at once by a blank wall of ignorance on his part."

Mrs. Bligh is again silent. Her own small experience of the young man has tallied too completely with the opinion now expressed by her companion for her to be able honestly to controvert it; and yet she feels a vague sense of regret at having been the means of opening the disdainful young eyes beside her to their old playfellow's shortcomings. They sit for awhile in mute quiet on their sunny bench; and some militia, who, when they arrived, had been drilling in the green close, making a scarlet splash against the sobriety of the low - toned masonry, depart, and leave the place to their undisputed possession.

"And yet there is something to be said for him too!" continues Pamela presently, the pendulum of her judgment beginning to swing towards the other direction as it becomes evident that no remonstrance against her unflattering estimate of her admirer is forthcoming; "he has a good deal of natural shrewdness; he manages all the business of the Tandem and Lifeboat Clubs. I have known him all my life, so that I should have nothing to find out; his conduct to that old pig, his father, who has blasted his life, is simply angelic; and I do not suppose if I lived to be a hundred that I should ever have such a solid block of devotion offered to me again."

At the beginning of this speech, Anne has felt inclined to laugh at the singularly slender and unattractive list of attractions so dispassionately put forth, but at the end she grows grave. " A solid block of devotion!" Judging from the very few and small chips that have ever fallen to her own share, a woman would indeed be wise to think long and weigh nicely ere she rejected a whole " block." And yet——

" If the fors and againsts of any course of action were not so inextricably mixed, how much simpler life would be !" cries the girl impatiently.

"Well," says Mrs. Bligh caustically, yet not unkindly, " I suppose that since you approach the subject in so business-like a spirit, all you have to do is to take out your scales and see which kick the beam, the pros or the cons ; which weighs heaviest : his want of book-learning, or his management of the Tandem Club ; the narrowness of his horizon, or the depth of his heart ?"

Pamela's cheek grows a shade nearer in hue to her fresh lips at the slight sarcasm of her friend's tone, but after a minute she rejoins impulsively :

" I will abide by your decision, then! It
was you who first opened my eyes to his
deficiencies. Heaven knows, poor fellow,
they are obvious enough—but I did not
see them, or they did not seem to matter,
till you pointed them out!—you shall make
up my mind for me."

" *I!*"—with an accent of the strongest and
most horrified negation—" not for worlds!"

" They all wish it so much, poor dears!"—
says Pamela, in a voice of the utmost per-
plexity, pushing up her hat and her curly
hair, and revealing a quarter of an inch more
of charming low square brow ; not, as in the
case of many people who unwittingly dis-
place their fringe, half a yard of disguised
high forehead—" even Sue, even Fezy "—
laughing distressfully—" are learning to disappear noiselessly out of any room in which
George and I happen to be together ; and
though I have run him down so much to
you,—it was very mean of me, but after you
called him a dreadful bore so much as a
matter of course I was ashamed to own that

I saw anything in him,—but all the same I have a sneaking sort of kindness for him; sometimes I think it is not so very sneaking, and then at other times it seems to dwindle to nothing.   I suppose"—with a troubled look of appeal—"one ought by rights to feel something quite different — something headlong."

Anne laughs.

"That epithet can certainly scarcely be applied to your sentiment as you describe it."

Pamela joins in the laugh, but vexedly. "It does sound unutterably tame, does not it? but yet at one time it did very well.   I believe it would have gone on doing very well if I had not seen—become acquainted with—no, not so much as that, but just got a glimpse of—something far different—something, oh, how much better!"

Her eyes are bent on the ground, but more in thoughtfulness than confusion, nor is there any variation of colour or flutter of voice to justify the outrageous pang of fear that clutches the elder woman by the throat at the innocently-meant words. There is a silence. The lion wind of March has penetrated, but translated into a lamb, even this retired corner. How gently he is running over the ivy branches, wagging them as he goes. The girl looks up suddenly with excited resolution in her blooming face.

" Since it is you who have showed me that better—that different—yes, do you think I have not seen the reflection of it in your face all these days?—you shall decide for me. I have told you as well as I can how I feel. I am not very happy at home, as you know; I rather wish to marry; I know that he would be my humble servant all his life; and I really do like him—in a way! But is that enough? If you say yes, it shall be yes; if you say no, it shall be no! Now, which is it to be?"

She has turned her lovely countenance, becomingly animated yet not deeply moved, fully towards her companion, and awaits her answer with a serious smile. Anne averts her face. Since it is apparently a dial-plate

on which her emotions are written with such
lamentable plainness, her young friend shall
not, at all events, have the opportunity of
reading the strong temptation now legibly
written upon it; the temptation to accept
the power over another's destiny thus thrust
into her hand, to give the advice which to
many unprejudiced persons would seem the
best possible under the circumstances ; would
pronounce that Yes which, in addition to
wafting this exquisite little bark into a safe
and weather-tight harbour for life, would also
— even to her own soul she scarcely formulates that "also."   If George Mulholland
take Pamela Capel-Smith to wife, there is
not the slightest doubt that she will never
pose either as a Nereid or as any other 'id
or 'ad to Sir Robert Coke.   She remains so
long silent, and with averted head, that
Pamela loses patience.

    " I do not believe that you are paying the
smallest heed to what I am saying," she cries
reproachfully.   "Oh, do please answer, one
way or the other."

Then, since it can no longer be avoided, Mrs. Bligh turns her face—to the girl's surprise a deeply troubled one—upon her questioner.

"How can you ask such a thing?" she says sternly. "How dare you try to thrust upon me such a responsibility?"

Pamela droops the corners of her mouth like a scolded child.

"You refuse, then?"

"Undoubtedly I do!" with a stringent and indignant emphasis.

"Absolutely?"

"More than absolutely, if there can be more!"

The other sighs impatiently, and for a minute or two looks extremely downcast. Then her countenance clears.

"I will decide it by drawing lots!" she cries triumphantly; "that is as good a way as any other; and at least you will not object to holding them?"

As she speaks she stoops and picks two of the grass blades—fine and dainty, as is ever the herbage in these unploughed feudal closes—and measuring them carefully together, pinches off half the stalk of one to make it conspicuously shorter than the other; and having done so, unclasps the reluctant fingers of one of her friend's hands and forces the two blades between them.

" There!" turning away her head, and screwing up her eyes ; " I will not look till you have arranged them. You understand : the long one is George ; the short one "—her voice involuntarily taking on a tone of greater alacrity—" is no George. Are you ready ?"

Mechanically Anne obeys, and holds out her clenched hand, in which the two fateful grasses are sitting with their green heads exactly and deceptively on a level. In a second Pamela has whipped out—the long one.

" Then it is to be George !" she says, in a rather flat voice, which, if it expresses no dismay, certainly evidences no elation. The elation, if it exists, is elsewhere. Anne's

heart has given an ungovernable spring of
relief and satisfaction in the answer thus
rendered by blind fortune to the appeal
addressed to her.

But that throb of keen and unalloyed
pleasure has but a moment's life. At the
sight of the delicate and brilliant creature
beside her, thus indifferently tossing herself
and her possibilities away to so unequal a
destiny, a wave of perhaps unnecessary remorse—since, after all, she has been only
passively instrumental in the decision—
sweeps over Mrs. Bligh. With an impulse
of possibly quixotic generosity, and a gesture
of revolt all the more decided because it is
the result of a victory over her own interests,
she snatches the grass blade, which the
other is still thoughtfully eyeing, out of her
hand, and tosses it to the spring breeze.

" It is not George !" she says, in a low
and troubled, but emphatic voice. " It shall
not, and can't be George ! I refused just
now to interfere ; I know that ; but "—with
ever-rising agitation—" it is impossible—I

should be committing a crime if I let you.
You do not care a straw about him. Would
you have taken such a way of deciding if you
had? He is not the least worthy of you,"
her excitement increasing as the image of
George, dull, sulky, and provincial, rises
before her mind's eye—"What a fool you
must be, not to see that you are meat for his
masters!"

  *   *   *   *   *

The week, but young when the foregoing
conversation was held, has run out. It is
Sunday morning, and against the obscured
window-panes the rain is smartly dashing.
At a table in the school-room window Mrs.
Mulholland, with Concordance and Bible
open before her, is helping Sue to prepare
that portion of Scripture, her exegesis of
which is shortly—weather permitting— to be
imparted to a class of small Welsh scholars at
the Sunday-school. The little girl is listening, amiable but bored, and with an anxious
eye covertly cast on the weather.

"Oh, mother!" cries she presently, in a

distressed voice, " I am so afraid it is going to clear."

" Afraid!" repeats Mrs. Bligh, who is also present, looking up with lifted eyebrows from her book. " I am sure I hope it is. I do not at all agree with you, Sue."

" Ah! but you have not to teach in the Sunday-school," replies Sue, with a heavy sigh.

Mrs. Bligh laughs. " No, I own that would alter my views of the weather a good deal."

" I was in great luck last year," rejoins the child, encouraged by this unexpected sympathy from a grown-up person. " I had seven quite wet Sundays. Oh, how I hope it is not going to clear!"

But the ardour of this aspiration does not, as some optimists would have us believe, procure its fulfilment. The rain veil draws away from the earth just in time for the infant Cymri to receive the benefit of whatever new lights upon the subject of Joseph and his Brethren can be struck out of the

combined efforts of Sue, her mother, and
Fezy. The part taken by the latter has
indeed been confined to standing on the sofa
with one paw laid on the Concordance and
mumbling the fingers held out to wave him
off, with the little white pearls his teeth, but
all so gently and airily that it would need a
heart of stone—a heart, at all events, a good
deal harder than Sue's—to rebuff him.

By the afternoon, thanks to a drying wind,
it is fine enough for Mrs. Bligh and her
hostess to stroll together along the high-
running private road, through their neighbour's park, the right to frequent which is
one of the most continual themes of Mrs.
Mulholland's gratitude and her husband's
brag. They have sat down on a now sunny
bench which for back has the quarried rock,
over whose crest great gorse bushes, all
aflower, are hanging out their oriflammes.
From their point of vantage, on what a fair
prospect their eyes may feed ! turn'ng from
where, on the extreme left, a long straight line
of foam stretching from the mainland to little

Puffin Island shows where the Dutchman's Bank—that fatal sandbank on which more than one vessel has found her death—lies right across the sea, to where, on the right, intervening trees hide out the graceful Menai Suspension Bridge. Between lie, and stand and curve, the range of moderately heighted, delicately varied Carnarvonshire mountains. Lying in the bosom of the highest twain, one divines, without seeing it, a little dark lake. Anne's eyes are full of the quiet yet deep pleasure of the true sea and mountain lover, but her companion's might be fixed upon the Cromwell Road, and the Natural History Museum, for all the enjoyment they express.

" I wish Czar had come with us," she says uneasily. "If you had pressed him a little more, I think he would. It might have distracted his thoughts."

" He does not care much about scenery, does he ?"

" Oh, I do not know. About as much as other people, I dare say. But I was not

14

thinking of the scenery ; I feel as if he ought not to be left to brood upon his own sad thoughts. I had no idea that he would have taken it so much to heart."

" No more had I."

" I knew that he was always fond of Pamela"—visions of an old Satyr jumping out of stair-corners start involuntarily before the listener's eye—"indeed, she was often rather silly about it, and misunderstood him when he only meant to be kind. But even I had no notion of how much his heart was set upon the marriage. In some ways I think he is more to be pitied than even George."

Anne raises her eyebrows. "I do not think I can go quite so far as that."

"Young people get over anything ; but he, poor darling, though he looks so boyish, of course is not young really, and he has taken it *dreadfully* to heart. You see, between ourselves—I talk openly to you, because I know how entirely you are on our side"— (Mrs. Bligh winces.) " Pamela's little independence would have made it all plain-sailing. He frets sadly at not being able to do more for George."

She pauses expectantly, and Mrs. Bligh is aware that some slight sign of admiration for such paternal tenderness is expected of her. But the recollection of the dinners at Bignon, and the Chat Noir, as reported by Pamela, are too recent in her mind to make any such utterance possible. She looks away uneasily towards the tallest hill, round whose head a scarf of vapour is twisted, and thence drops her eyes upon the lower range, with their network of stone walls, and their little dark-green woods sunk in hollows.

"It was a thunderbolt, nothing less to us all," continues Mrs. Mulholland. "We had always looked upon it as a certainty. I am sure you must have heard me a hundred times tell her that she was one of the family."

"Yes, I have often heard you say so."

"I really thought she was; we all took it for granted. It shows "—disconsolately—

"that one ought never to take anything for granted. But ever since she arrived this time, I have seen a difference, a coldness. One might really imagine that she must have heard something against George, against his character. And yet I am sure there is no young man whose life could better bear being looked into. Czar often laughs at him for being so old-maidish, but then "— in a tone from which the element of pride is by no means absent—" I imagine that he had a *jeunesse* very *orageuse*."

The speaker's troubled eyes are fixed in all innocence, and with no intention beyond a vague desire for sympathy, upon her listener's. But to the latter's guilty consciousness there seems to be a questioning suspicion in them. She can for the moment frame no rejoinder. But her friend does not miss it. With her nose down, like a questing hound, she is following the trail of the idea started by herself.

" Do you think it is possible that anyone could have set her against him ? But no !

what motive could anyone have for being so malicious? You are the only person she is likely to have discussed him with, and "— with a smile at the ludicrous improbability of the suggestion—" I scarcely suspect *you* of having done us such an ill turn. *You*" —affectionately—" would have given us a helping hand, if you could, *that* I am sure of."

These words, and the tone of simple sincerity in which they are uttered, effectually as they remove the alarm under which Mrs. Bligh had just been labouring, do not make her feel more comfortable. She avoids her companion's confident glance, and looks straight before her, across the Strait, to the sweet narrow valley of Aber, and the bluff headland of Penmaen-Mawr.

" In such cases no one has any business either to help or hinder," she says trenchantly.

CHAPTER XI.

Long before a se'nnight has passed since
the departure of Pamela—who had wisely
fled immediately upon the springing of her
mine—Mrs. Bligh's action has changed its
aspect in her own eyes, from one of heroism
to that of treachery. She would have dearly
liked to have accompanied her young friend
in her exodus, but she stays behind as a
sort of expiation. To a nature frank to a
fault and open to a misfortune, the daily and
hourly dissimulation entailed by the guileless
confidence of the Mulholland family in her
sympathy, and by the certainty that they
express a hundred times a day of her wish
to help them if she could to the desired goal,
is a punishment and a trial almost beyond

her powers. Scores of times she has all but yielded to the temptation of bringing down a new thunderbolt; of springing a second mine, by crying out, "You have to thank me for it! It was I that did it!" Scores of times she has begun a sentence, the end of which must send her to pack up her box in hopeless estrangement from the little group now hanging so affectionately around her. And scores of times the sentence has dwindled away unfinished—the match has gone out, the determination has died; killed partly by the difficulty and pain of forcing any suspicion into minds so absolutely and obtusely unsuspecting; and secondly by the entire hopelessness of conveying to any intelligence a comprehension of the grotesque and distorted generosity which had dictated her action.

That she had counselled Pamela to reject George, because she herself was particularly anxious that she should marry him; though the exact and naked truth is so far more incredible than any lies, that it would be impossible to gain credence for the statement without further explanation, the mere distant self-suggestion of which makes her writhe. And so, through the lengthening spring days —in strolls among the quickening trees, and by the breeze-swept sea ; in tedious threshings-out of the subject over needlework by day, and endless lamentations over bedroom fires at night—she works out her atonement.

Mrs. Mulholland's topics of conversation have never been very numerous, as, indeed, they cannot be in the case of a person of extremely limited intelligence and a monotonous life ; but now to her tormented and guilty brain it seems that the one voracious theme of Pamela's mysterious crime has swallowed up all its scanty brethren. It is discussed, in all its bearings, from morning to night ; but the favourite mode of treatment, and the one which tries most severely the auditor's nerves, consists of a never-ending series of speculations upon the whose and the why of that malevolent influence which

had wrought the baneful metamorphosis. It
is not only from the friend of her school-
days, but from the whole of the family, with
the exception of the main sufferer, that she
has to bear the brunt of the maledictions
launched with such heartiness and unanimity
against the unknown author of the family
misfortune; maledictions in which she is
called upon so often to join that Richard III.'s
line is perpetually rising in her mind :

"Had I cursed now, I had cursed myself."

Twenty times a day she is obliged to curse
herself. Once, driven to desperation, she
has proposed an abridgment of her visit, a
return home, but has been met by such
piteous upbraidings and entreaties that no
course has been open to her but at once to
withdraw the suggestion.

"I do not know what would become of
Czar if you, too, left us. You are sure he
does not care about you ? Oh, come "—with
a light accent of reproach—" that is putting
the saddle on the wrong horse ; he is so sen-

sitive, he says he is sure you do not like him. I tell him it is only your manner—that you always had rather a short manner; but if you go—and the Lascelles away, too—he will have no motive for keeping up at all. You do not know how he droops and mopes when we are alone."

"Oh, don't I wish I could get hold of whoever it was that set her against us!" cries Lucile, with honest energy, "would not I punch his or her head? Dear pet!"—her eyes tenderly following her father's figure, seen through the window, walking with more pensiveness and less spring than usual along the garden path—"I declare it has made him look five years older. But even now, is not he wonderful for his age?"

"I do not think"—evasively—"that I quite know how old he is."

"Oh, no more do we exactly. He would not like us to."

"He tore the leaf out of the Bible that had his birthday on it," says Sue, in a rather lowered voice, "so I expect he is pretty old.

But is not he wonderful? His lovely hair, and his teeth all his own; at least"—with some stirrings of a compunctious veracity — " at least, a great many of them."

"We must all do our best to cheer him up," says Mrs. Mulholland, her glance, like her step-daughter's, pursuing the languid figure of the head of the house; " I was saying so to George. He went out this morning early to try and get him a widgeon for dinner; it is the only thing he seems to fancy."

" I should have thought that it was poor George himself who needed widgeons," says Anne drily.

But this is not the view taken by the family, nor, indeed, by the sufferer himself. With an angry and compunctious amazement Mrs. Bligh sees how entirely the young man —severely as his own dejected countenance and forced spirits show him to be suffering— enters into his relatives' views as to Czar's being the prime claims for sympathy and con- solation. It gives an even sharper edge to

the widow's remorse for her ill-judged interference to discover of what matter-of-fact self-
effacement, of what obscure heroism, he is
capable, whose future she has thought herself
justified in destroying, because he has a Welsh
accent; because he once confused the poet
Browning with a local ironmonger of the
same name; and because he had resented
with a not unnatural display of spirit her own
early incivility towards him. The result of
her compunctious reflections translates itself
directly into speech—speech addressed to her
victim's sister.

"How wonderfully well he bears it! How
plucky he is over it!"

"Yes, is not he?"—warmly. "It is *so*
unusual to have such spirits at his age."

"At *his* age? Why, he cannot be more
than four-and-twenty."

"*Czar not more than four-and-twenty!*"
with a burst of astonished laughter.

"Czar! Who was talking of Czar? I
spoke of George."

"Oh, George, poor fellow! Yes "—with

less enthusiasm—"it is good of him. He tries to keep up for Czar's sake."

"You certainly are the most devoted son and daughter that ever man was blessed with!" says Anne, in a tone the profound astonishment expressed in which she is herself not quite aware of.

"It would be very odd if we were not," returns Lucile, with emotion; "never in all our lives can one of us remember his having spoken crossly to us. What other father jumps up to open the door for his own daughter as he did for me last night? And if he *has* to say anything disagreeable to us it hurts him a great deal more than it hurts us. When he told George last autumn that he could not let him go with the Lascelles to Scotland because it was impossible for him to afford him any money to tip the keepers, the tears literally rolled down his cheeks. George told me so himself."

Anne sinks into a marvelling silence, pondering upon the strangeness of human nature; upon how little solid virtues or

benefits avail to gain its oddly-built affec-
tions, and upon the incomprehensibility of
the cult produced in these honest and simple
hearts by an egotist, who can win their eager
consent to his gnawing of their patrimony
and suppression of their rightful pleasures
by a few blathering phrases and crocodile
tears. Her remorse towards the family
takes several different shapes. The first is
a warmly-urged invitation—addressed both
to the girl herself and to her mother—to
Lucile, to pay her a long visit in Tite Street,
with a view to getting those helps towards
the cultivation of her talent which her father
has tearfully explained himself unable to give
her.

"My little house and I are so useless,"
Anne has said rather ruefully; "I should
be so glad if I could feel that either of us
was doing any good to our fellow-creatures."

And when the girl has responded with
sparkling eyes and phrases of exaggerated
yet evidently genuine gratitude, Mrs. Bligh's
conscience—such is our leniency to ourselves

—already feels itself a little eased of its burden. Another and much more irksome form of her expiation is the joining with his family in their attempts to raise Czar's spirits, the best means of attaining which would apparently lie in inducing him—no hard task —to talk about his past life, and about the wholesale ravages among the female sex which, according to his own implication, have characterized it. When she has listened with complacency for the third time to that anecdote which relates how, being in a four-wheeled cab with a matron —over his relations to whom he chuckles a good deal—he recognised in the driver the fair one's infuriated husband, and yet had the presence of mind to put into his hand his fare without any sign of conscious-ness—when, I say, she has listened with a smile of approbation for the third time to this choice study in ethics, she feels as if her debt were, indeed, all but wiped off. With George himself it is true her efforts are not crowned with that success which marks her intercourse with his kin. Though it is apparent from their manner to her, and their reiterated assurances of confidence in her good will, that he has not imparted his suspicions to them, yet she feels that if he does not absolutely know—as how could he?—yet that he divines whose has been the adverse influence which has laid low his hopes. She has made several shy efforts—very difficult to a reserved and self-conscious woman—to approach him in a propitiatory spirit, but has been invariably met by a rebuff—a rebuff that in her normal state would have driven her to a stinging retort, but compunction has made her humble, and sends her back to repeat her spurned endeavour. One evening, seeing him sitting with both hands clutching his forehead, as he bends over an odd volume of Browning, accidentally left behind by Pamela—poor fellow! it is clear that he has felt his blunder about the ironmonger—she edges her chair diffidently near him, and stealing a glance over his shoulder at the open page of the

"Ring and the Book," a poem no doubt selected by him for the misleading simplicity of its title, she says :

"You have chosen rather a hard nut to crack. If you would let me, I think I could pick you out something easier for a beginner.'

He starts, not having been aware of her neighbourhood.

"Thank you," he says brusquely. "It would be a waste of time; he is a cut above me! I had better stick to what I understand," ostentatiously tossing away the book, and picking up the *Pink 'Un.*

She draws off, red and abashed. But if his rudeness is hard to bear, his kindness is far worse. She is moved to tears of compunction, when on the day before her departure —they let her go at last—he awkwardly presents her with a basket of plovers' eggs, gathered expressly for her, with a mumbled intimation that she had said she was fond of them. It is very stupid of her, but the guilty tears literally spring to her eyes.

"For me? You got them on purpose for
me! Oh, how wonderfully, how *immensely*
kind of you!"

The acknowledgment sounds to an unin-
structed ear so ludicrously out of proportion
to the benefit bestowed, that Mrs. Mulholland breaks into a laugh.

"Why, Nan, you could not be more
obliged to him if he had saved your life!"

"He likes doing things for other people!"
adds Lucile, with a loving look at her brother,
"and besides"—pressing Anne's hand mean-
ingly—"he knows that you would get us
rocs' eggs if you could; do not you,
George?"

It is the day before her departure, as I
have said. The spring—so long has she
been their guest—is, unlike Christabel's
coming, "quickly" up this way. It seems
a sin to leave these burgeoning woods before
the blue of their hyacinth flooring has burst
from its green cradle; and yet, wood and
hyacinth lover as Anne is, she feels a feverish
hurry to be back in her narrow town home,

little as it would seem that she has to return to. Between the two friends who parted from her now nearly a month ago and herself a wall of separation appears to have grown up. They afford her almost as little knowledge of the world into which they have flown back as did Noah obtain from his heartless raven. From Sir Robert Coke she has received a couple of notes, kindly and very nearly affectionately worded, but containing the minimum of information which even a man's letter can supply. The first is beautified in her eyes by a hope for her own speedy return. The second—but then he described himself as in great haste at the time of its penning--holds no such expression. She broods for days over the reason—doubtless there is none, save the hurry he alleged—for its omission. Nor is Pamela—usually to her friend an enthusiastic and exuberant correspondent—much less chary of her letters. She at least cannot have the excuse of crowded hours, and pressing work, justly alleged by the sculptor. Why is it, then, that her communications are so few, so short, and so dull? Only one bears a trace of her old effusiveness, and in that the expressions of enthusiasm usually applied to Mrs. Bligh are employed in describing a Sunday spent by Miss Capel-Smith at a country house, which she seems to have enjoyed with an extravagant zest, of the cause for which she gives no adequate explanation. Over this, too, Anne puzzles long and anxiously. It may be that the girl has a delicacy in addressing letters to a house where the sight of her handwriting—formerly so frequent and so familiar—must need arouse painful feelings.

Well, speculation on the subject is useless, since, as Anne reflects with a sigh of relief, all will soon be explained. She smiles to herself at the agony-column phrase in which her thought has dressed itself. In four-and-twenty hours she will be back in Tite Street, and unless Pamela is more changed than she can possibly believe, she will be on the doorstep to receive her. Mrs. Bligh has

informed both her allies of her intended
return in a few jubilant lines; as to the man,
even to her own heart, she formulates no
express or definite hopes, but on the girl she
may count with a cheerful certainty. She
is so ashamed of her own almost undis-
guisable gladness in her approaching departure that she spends herself in compunctious
and most sincere offers of hospitality to the
whole Mulholland family. She repeats and
presses her invitation to Lucile in particular,
urging the fixing of an exact date for it.

"I have been writing to a Slade student
about you," she says eagerly, "and she tells
me that there is a studio in Gower Street
—Black is the artist's name—where they
paint animals from life. I will have it all
arranged by the time you come; of course"
—with a shade of embarrassment, and a
memory of Czar's crocodile tears—"you shall
be put to no expense."

But to her surprise, her proposal, formerly
met by so effusive a welcome, now calls forth
only a confused and rueful evasion from the

girl, which is explained later by her stepmother.

"You see, Czar would not hear of it; he
is very, very much obliged to you; he says
that if he could bear to lie under an obliga-
tion to *any* one, it would be to you; but
even to you—I assure you, you are a great
favourite, though you will not believe it—he
cannot! It is his wonderfully proud, lofty
sort of nature. He says it would break his
heart to think that his children were being
pauperized!"

It is, therefore, with a debt quite unliqui-
dated, and a conscience a good deal more
heavily loaded than the omnibus which carries
her and her moderate possessions, that Anne
departs. George drives her to the station, as
he had driven her from it on her arrival,
almost five weeks ago; he escorts her,
despite her protestations, to the platform,
nor does he leave her till her train is well
in motion. He does it all with an iron air
of duty, which does not add to her ease in
receiving his civilities. It is not till she is

really seated in her carriage, and he is standing conscientiously beside the door till the
parting whistle releases him,·that she finds
courage to say :

"If ever you want to run up for a night
or two, you will not forget Tite Street? It
is not so *very* out-of-the-way, whatever Czar
may say !"

There is in her own ears something self-
betrayingly compunctious in her tone, and
perhaps he notices it. He only answers :

"Thank you, but I am not likely to be
in London;" and then—the guard waving
his flag—the young man takes off his hat
with an honestly struggled-with air of relief,
and in a minute more she has lost sight
of him.

Up to the last moment she had cherished
vague intentions of confessing herself to
him, of offering to try to undo the ill she
has done him ; but now it is too late. Her
country outing is over, and she may look
back upon it, and upon the mode she has
chosen of manifesting her gratitude for the

simple and hearty hospitality offered her, with what satisfaction she may. Remorse holds undisputed sway over her mind till Chester, then expectation begins to elbow it a little aside, and has successfully shoved it off the scene by the time, towards seven o'clock in the evening, that she and her dusty belongings drive up to her own little green door.

Pamela is not on the doorstep ; that is not very surprising, since the exact moment of the traveller's arrival cannot be known ; and a London doorstep is not a place suitable for making a prolonged stay on. But neither, when the thrilling of the electric bell has brought a *sémillante* parlourmaid in an embroidered apron to the door, does there appear any sign of a visitor within. For these can hardly be called visitors, these two fawn-coloured and one iron-gray person, who are saying, " How do you do ?" in so very loud a voice from the stairfoot. Their barks are soon turned into squeaks of pleasurable recognition ; that is, Sall's and Tory's are.

As for poor Twankle, his memory is as small as his tiny body, and he has to own that he cannot quite put a name to her.

She explains herself hurriedly to him, and pushing them all gently aside, makes her way to the hall-table, and casts an eager glance over the notes and letters—not very numerous—which await her there. Her first impression is one of disappointment. In Coke's handwriting there is nothing, and though there is a letter with Pamela's superscription, yet a country post-mark, which her eye at once perceives, tells her that of the looked-for meeting with her to-day there is no chance. The note—it is no more—when opened, confirms and deepens the defeated feeling that its outside had inspired. Miss Capel-Smith has gone out of town for the inside of a week, and though her letter is full of expressions of regret at not being at home to welcome back her friend, yet to that friend's mind the words convey no adequate explanation of the "why" of a departure which so oddly coincides with her own arrival. She is too chilled in spirit to care for the moment to open the two or three other missives addressed to her, but, gathering them carelessly up, mounts the stairs with her still agitated escort of wagging tails, and smirking muzzles, and enters her drawing-room.

Its look of rigidly neat fireless emptiness damps her still more than she already is. Accustomed to the lavish crowd of country blossoms in the Mulholland drawing-room, it looks nudely flowerless. Her palms—she fingers them discontentedly—have not been sponged since her departure, have been over-watered, and look sick and yellow. Her husband's *chaise longue*, memento of the long years of his agony, and her ordeal, always an unsightly object, too big for the little room, has been pulled more forward than usual. She gives it an irritated shove back, and then with a remorseful change of mood restores it to its position of prominence. As she stands looking disconsolately round at her well-soaped and beeswaxed, but melan-

choly little monarchy, she asks herself what
there was in so dismal a home-coming to
look forward to. With a shiver—late April
as it is, the evenings are still raw—she drops
on her knees before the fireplace, and puts a
match to the sticks. As they break into a
sudden cold little blaze, she draws up the
pouf on which—it flashes across her suddenly
—Coke had sat at her feet on his last visit,
and sinks down upon it. On that evening
she had expected him as little as she does
now, possibly then——

To check so unwise a train of thought she
opens the letters still lying neglected in her
hand. The first is the prospectus of a mine ;
the second is a request from a philanthropic
acquaintance, to take the place of a fellow-
worker fallen ill, and accompany the writer
to a "happy evening" for factory girls at
Poplar, on the ensuing Monday ; the third
and last is a bidding from Lady St. George,
the giver of the luncheon at which she had
begun her course of ill-usage of young Mulholland, to dine with her, on the invitation of

a member of the Government, at the House
of Commons on the following day. She
throws the mine into the fire, and promptly
writes acceptances of the other two.

An eager desire has seized her to fill her
empty life with something, whether philanthropy or social pleasures is a matter of
detail compared with the main object of
filling the useless vacuity of her existence.
It had not seemed either so void or so profit-
less on her journey, either at Chester or even
at Willesden or Euston, as it does to her
to-night, sitting in flat disappointment, with
her feet on her brass fender. Though of
late she has been counting the hours till her
departure thence, she goes nigh now to wish-
ing herself back at Plas Drow; to be again
seeing and hearing Jim the terrier gallop
down the long drawing-room with the hearth-
brush, which it is his nightly privilege to have
thrown for him to pursue and worry, and
then return with it into his basket, to bite
yet a few more bristles off. She thinks
almost affectionately even of Czar. " I have

fallen so low that I should be quite glad to
hear once more the tale of the four-wheeler
and the infuriated husband." She says it
out loud, and laughs.

Morning brings a brighter mood, but
neither it, nor noon, nor afternoon bring any
tidings of the sculptor. A postman has just
gone by, empty-handed for her, when the
arrival of Lady St. George, and her
brougham, to convey her to the proposed
entertainment, happily diverts her thoughts
into a different channel.

Lady St. George asks her how she has
enjoyed herself in the country, but is in too
great a hurry to tell her of her own next
Sunday luncheon, which is to include the
Bishop of the Andaman Islands, and the
strong man from the Aquarium, to listen to
the answer. The theme lasts till they reach
their destination, and after a walk and climb
of about a mile and a half through the im-
measurable passages of the House, find
themselves in that black hole reserved for
the ladies. It is a new experience to Anne,

and she leans eagerly over the shoulders of
the fortunate occupiers of the front seats, to
peer through the grating at the ranks of
legislators lounging so cavalierly below.
Without remembering her want of acquaintance with her neighbours, she puts excited
questions to them, as to the identity of this
or that one. A prominent member of the
Opposition, with a mixed gift of waggery
and Billingsgate, is up, and is "slating" an
occupant of the Treasury Bench exactly opposite him, who, leaning comfortably back,
is listening with a smile of placid enjoyment
to a statement larded with suitable pleasantries,
to the effect that his mendacity is only equalled
by his imbecility. When the orator has sat
down to the music of profuse Hibernian
cheers, Lady St. George and her visitor
descend, guided by their intending host, to a
small and inconvenient room, where they
are presently joined by two or three smart
women, three or four well-known men, and
later, to Anne's astonishment, by the two
combatants in the war of words she has just

witnessed.   As they enter, the object of
attack is patting his assailant friendlily on the
shoulder, and saying in a congratulatory tone,
" You were in capital form to-night."

CHAPTER XII.

MRS. BLIGH has never before dined at the House of Commons, that justly popular form of social enjoyment, whose popularity sufficiently disposes of any accusation brought against the British upper classes of being the slaves of their pampered palates, since they cheerfully exchange their own *chefs* and vintages for a worse cooked and served and waited-on dinner than falls to the lot of many meaner persons. But, then, no ducal mansion boasts such an after-dinner promenade as the Terrace of the House of Commons.

There is about these dinners something of the scrambling charm of a picnic, and also — which no other picnic can afford — a gratifying sense that you are helping to govern your country, when, at the sound of the division bell, the men of your party, with pushed-back chairs and thrown-down dinner-napkins, fly from their tough mutton to the legislative arena. None of the guests are known to Anne, except by reputation, although by the time the feast is half over she has made out that one face which has struck her as not quite unfamiliar is that of the diplomat of Lady St. George's Sunday luncheon, who had told one of the good stories of which George Mulholland had amputated the point for her; and who had appeared to be an intimate of Sir Robert Coke's; perhaps from him she may glean some information about her strangely silent Lion. She has already—sheltered by the kindly gloom of the brougham—hesitated a question to Lady St. George as to whether she has lately seen him. Her answer has been an absent and careless negative, followed by a much more animated counter-query, as to Mrs. Bligh's opinion upon the possibility of capturing the sculptor for the

Bishop and the strong man next Sunday. The Diplomat is not near Anne at dinner, but afterwards on the Terrace her opportunity comes. She is standing alone gazing over the balustrade at the river, when, since no one is talking to her, and he rather likes her look, he civilly addresses her.

" You have never done this kind of thing before, I think I heard you say."

" Never !" then changing the subject with abrupt fear of letting her moment slip, she adds hurriedly, " I think you had the pleasure—I mean "—laughing confusedly—" I think I had the pleasure of meeting you at luncheon at Lady St. George's about six weeks ago."

He has not the faintest recollection of having ever set eyes upon her before tonight, but he has not led Cotillons in Vienna and Paris for twenty years for nothing ; so he replies with a bow and a smile that he is not very likely to have forgotten anything so agreeable.

" We have an acquaintance in common !"

she says, still rushing at her fences—" Sir Robert Coke."

"Coke!" in a tone of relief and pleasure, "dear old chap! do you know him? Let us have a little talk about him! do you mind," turning up his coat collar and shivering. " walking up and down a bit? Thames breezes are not exactly Zephyrs. And so you know dear old Coke?—charming artist, is not he? One or two of his things *very nearly* great, just something wanting. People say ill-natured things about him, of course; that he is played out, and Rococo, and that the ' Equestrian H.R.H.,' which got him his Baronetcy, has some startling anatomical novelties, ha! ha!"

As she does not join in his mirth he arrests it, and continues more gravely:

" That is envy, pure envy, of course, but I wish he would stop their mouths with something indubitable, instead of the catchpenny prettinesses he has been giving us of late."

Catchpenny prettinesses! The thought

flashes across the listener's mind whether the bust of old Sir Peter Mammon, taken from a cast after death, is likely to come under the head of a "prettiness," whether catchpenny or otherwise; but the fancy is only a momentary one, and gives way at once to the immense and painful surprise caused by her companion's words. It is the very first time that the idea has been presented to her that her friend's talent can be disputed or his achievements held to be on the wane. The combined novelty and unpleasantness of the suggestion make her incapable of speech, incapable, too, of appreciating the noble terrace she is pacing, the "huge and thoughtful night" above her head, the towering Gothic height of the House on her left hand, or the dark river full of lovely reflections on her right. They have almost reached that end on which the Speaker's house abuts, and on which—happy Speaker—one of his drawing-room windows gives, before Mrs. Bligh's companion, seeing that he is not going to get any rejoinder out of her, resumes:

" The fact is he wants an inspiration ; he is too comfortable ; he needs an emotion of some kind to jog him out of his routine. If he could get something or someone to stir him up, he might do a big thing yet ; people say no ; that it is too late, but I do not hold with them. I believe in him, dear old chap! I told him so the other day when I met him at ——."

Mrs. Bligh starts. The name of the country house mentioned is the same as that where Miss Capel-Smith had described herself passing that Sunday, her prodigious enjoyment of which had puzzled Anne.

" When did you meet him at ——?" she asks hastily.

" Oh, two or three Sundays ago "—seeming surprised at the eager look with which she accompanies her question—" I cannot recollect the precise date."

" Was it a pleasant party ?"

Again he looks surprised at a something unnecessarily serious and urgent in her tone.

"Was it —— ?"

"I declare I forget ; nothing very wonderful, I imagine ; Coke"—beginning to laugh—"seemed to enjoy it."

A sort of foreboding of the cause of Coke's enjoyment seems to close Anne's throat, but, without further questioning, her interlocutor proceeds to explain himself.

"Our hostess had got hold of a very lovely young lady. I am bound to say we were all rather on the *qui vive* about her, and Coke—you know his partiality for your sex—was very much at her feet."

"Yes !"

"It was all in the way of business, of course"—his mirth rising again—"he was importuning her to sit to him for a Venus or a nymph, or something. I never saw him so much in earnest about anything in my life."

"Yes !"

"But the fair one was obdurate ; she looked demure, and said she did not think her mamma would like it. I am not sure that her mamma was not right. Ah! there is Lady Olivia Z——" as a fat and heavy-looking girl accompanied by a couple of men comes within eyeshot. "They call her Beef Olive. How do you do, Lady Olivia?" . . .

There is something always disturbing to the mental equilibrium in an entirely new idea, and perhaps it is the absolute novelty to her of the suggestion of her friend's reputed decadence in his art that gives Mrs. Bligh such an uneasy night.

"Played out," "Rococo," "Catchpenny prettinesses." The objectionable phrases buzz in her ears and brain, as she tosses about in unhappy wakefulness, or slips off into worrying dreams. But the new idea, after all, has not the whole stage to itself. It is pushing aside, and again pushed aside, by one that is by no means new. "Very much at her feet." "Never saw him so much in earnest about anything in my life."

These phrases are but the expression of a notion which has lain sometimes latent—

sometimes more than latent—in Anne's own
mind. And then the two ideas, the new and
the old one, having tormented her separately,
join in a combined attack upon her, " What
he needs is an inspiration." " If he could
get hold of an emotion of some kind, he
might yet do something big!" And surely
if he never was so much in earnest in his
life, as in the endeavour to persuade Pamela
to lend her shy loveliness to his chisel, he
must be within hail of that very emotion,
which, in the opinion of one long intimate
with him, may be his artistic salvation. Is
he conscious of this himself? If so, is it not
the bounden duty of anyone who wishes him
well, of anyone to whom his interest is nearer
and dearer than her own, to aid him to the
utmost of her power ? If he is not conscious
of what would work so greatly to his advantage, is not it the bounden though still harder
duty of the supposed well-wisher to point
him out the path which, set with roses, yet
leads straight to the desired goal of his own
glory ?

The disagreeable duties, that in the small black hues of the night loom so great and undoubted are apt, when morning comes, to lose a good deal of their size and stringency, and during her dressing, breakfast and fore-noon a good deal of uncertainty as to her own future action sways Mrs. Bligh's dis-turbed heart and mind ; but through the early afternoon the puritan-spirited formula, " It must be right, because it is so disagree-able," goes on gaining in convincingness, until at four o'clock she puts herself into a hansom for fear lest, if she trust herself to walk, her resolution may break down, and gives the address of Sir Robert Coke's studio. It is the first time that she has intruded upon him uninvited, and though he has frequently reproached her for not visiting him oftener, and begged her in general terms to repair the omission in the future, yet the nearer she draws to her destination—her Shrewsbury and Talbot hansom conveys her undesirably fast—the more general those terms seem to have been, and the less to

justify any special invasion. Probably he
has a model, or is engaged with some royalty
or millionaire, or, worst of all, with some
more favoured female friend, in his *tête-à-tête*
with whom she is about to intrude her un-
asked and undesired presence.

Coke's studio, or rather studios—for his
extensive *clientèle* has long ago obliged him
to overflow the limits of his original *atelier*—
stands back from the street; and after dis-
missing her cab, Mrs. Bligh has to cross a
small slip of smutty grass, ornamented with a
coal-black town tree, to reach it. In the brief
transit her courage falls so low that, but for
the accident of someone just happening to
issue from the general door of the block—an
accidental someone who would witness and
marvel at her flight—she would turn tail
even now. Besides the little forecourt, she
has—when once inside—a long corridor still
to traverse, as the door at which he has in-
structed her to ring—the door of the studio,
where he himself models—away from the din
of his workmen's tools, and shut from the

inroads of the general public—is at the very
end of the passage. As she flits along that
passage, her eye rests on the casts of some of
his principal works, which stand on either
hand. The " Lioness and Cubs," which first
brought him into notice ; the " Dejanira and
Centaur," which was his first commission
from Royalty, etc. Surely — the belittling
phrase returning upon her memory—there is
no catchpenny prettiness about *them*.

She has reached the door, whose closed
aspect—although it is always closed—gives
her a fresh pang of misgiving, and rings the
bell with a shyness-born force which sets it
jangling for several moments—moments spent
by her in the too-late reflection of how much
more considerate and dignified it would have
been on her part to have rung the bell of the
larger and more public studio, and sent her
card by the head man to the sculptor. He
would then have had the option of escaping
her visit, if it is ill-timed. But she has now
left him no more choice in the matter than
has a fox tracked to its stopped earth.

The bell has just ceased its unnecessary length of clamour, when the door opens slowly, and, as it seems to the trembling candidate for admission, reluctantly, and the master of the demesne appears in the aperture. In the second that elapses before he recognises her, she has time to notice how ill he is looking; his features drawn as with pain, and his whole look giving a pulled-down impression. That impression disappears, or at least is greatly lessened next instant, when his whole mobile face lights up with a smile of friendly surprise and welcome; lights up with so bright a brightness as to shine down the traces of sickness and suffering which at first had been so legibly written upon it.

" My dear friend "—impulsively stretching out both hands, and then laughingly drawing them back—but then again holding them towards her, though beyond touching distance, to show her that clayey coating which forbids the pressure that his kind and gladdened eyes tell her he would like to give her fingers —" come in, come in ; this is too pleasant."

She gives a sigh of relief at so satisfactory a solution of her doubts, but a trace of lingering misgiving makes her still hesitate on the threshold and ask dubiously :

" Are you sure that it is quite correct ? That you have no model, no Rothschild, no crowned head in there ?"—peering beyond him and laughing nervously.

" You suspicious woman "—laying his hand in momentary forgetfulness of its condition on her shoulder, and gently urging her inwards ; " come in and see for yourself."

Then, indeed, yielding joyfully, she enters and follows him as he walks, keeping a little before her. She gives a second sigh of pleasure this time, when the inner door shuts her in from the noise of the outer world, into this pleasant-temperatured privacy ; where there are no eyes more prying than the sightless ones of the cast of the latest Venus —dug out of a Roman garden—to comment upon her action, which now seems fully justified by its success. She looks round her with an air of leisurely enjoyment upon the objects so familiar to her, though she has only been here two or three times before. The high carved wood mantelpiece, above which a procession of Greek filleted youths and maidens and priests is leading a " heifer lowing at the skies " to a flower-wreathed altar ; the charming little bronze group of the Erl-king snatching the boy out of his father's arms ; the very lay figure ; and the unfinished clay bust swathed in wet cloths—all, all are dear to her. From these her quick complacent glance returns to their owner. But it loses some of its satisfaction when the strong light pouring down from the top of the room shows her afresh the traces of illness on her friend's features, now that the transient, startled flush has left them. From his worn face her eye casually wanders downwards to his foot, whose limping she had already observed, and which she now perceives to be made unshapely by a list shoe.

"Now, madam !" he cries gaily, "are you

convinced that there is no little milliner behind the screen ?"

But she is too much occupied by the problem of that startling shoe to be able to answer in the same vein.

"What have you done to yourself?" she asks quickly—"what have you done to your foot ?"

He lifts his eyebrows, with a gesture of rueful humour.

"What have I done to my foot ? Say, rather, what has my grandfather's port wine done to it ? I, too, that am not at all sure I ever had a grandfather ?—do not look so tragic, my dear— but there is no use mincing matters ; I have had neither more nor less than a fit of the gout."

"*The gout !*"

There is consternation in her tone, for, indeed, it would have seemed to her almost as unlikely that the Vatican Apollo or the Diskobolos should have their immortal limbs swollen and disfigured by the old and ugly disorder indicated, as her spare and temperate friend. He laughs at the exaggeration of her tone.

"Yes, I have had my first memento — not *mori*, for I believe it does not kill one — but *senescere*, which "—with a shrug—"is worse. Do you think "—affectionately —"that, if I had not been such a poor old cripple, I should not have been on the doorstep of the dear little house to welcome you home? but "—with a half-tender, half-shamefaced intonation—"it is very cowardly of me ; but I had hopes I might have hidden my infirmities even from you yet a little longer."

She is still staring stupidly at that large loose shoe.

"It is no use," she says presently, looking up with a rather bewildered smile. "I have been trying hard, but I cannot get you and crutches to meet in my mind."

"Cannot you ?" with a somewhat gratified intonation.

"But I suppose you really have been quite ill—quite laid up ?"

" I have been learning what a jolly thing an old bachelor's sick-room is ;" then afraid— or she fancies so—of calling forth too pronounced an expression of sympathy for his lonely condition, he resumes hastily : " And as ill-luck always goes to ill-luck, the first day I was able to hobble down here I found in my letter-box a note from the man who bought my Marsyas—do you remember the Marsyas ?"

" No, it had left the studio before I first visited you."

"Well, a note from the fellow—he is a Sheffield scissors-maker—saying that, after mature consideration, he had come to the conclusion that the stain in the marble on the back of the statue is too bad for him to take it ; and if I can sell it he will bear half the loss."

" How very annoying !"

" More annoying than you think, little friend. He puts it upon the stain, but that is not his real reason."

" What is his real reason ?"

He sighs and passes his hand through

17

his hair, on which it leaves the imprint of clayey fingers.

"Have you ever reckoned among your acquaintances the number of people who dare to have an opinion of their own? Well, my scissors friend is not one of them. I can plainly read between the lines of his letter that he has come across the *critique* on my equestrian statue of H.R.H. in the *Times*. You have not seen it? I will send it you—in which the writer——"

"Well?"—breathlessly—"what does he say about you?"

"What does not he say?"—expressively— "let me think. That I have always been an impostor, and now, at last, I am an exposed one. That this statue in especial is only fit to ornament the top of a twelfth cake—that my Baronetcy was a disgraceful job—that——"

His hearer has gradually been growing more and more irefully hot at each clause of the enumeration; now she suddenly puts up her hands to her ears, crying :

" Stop — stop ! I will not hear any more."

Her eyes are brimming over with resentful tears, and her voice is choked. Her sympathy is sweet to him, but yet he feels a certain embarrassment at the violence of her expression of it—an embarrassment that prompts him to say in a tone that aims at being light and gay :

" But life is a system of balance and compensation ; on the very day I heard of the Marsyas, I got a so-and-so order for a reclining statue, so that I was something like the thief who summed up his day's work : 'Lost a clasp knife; stole a pocket-handkerchief ' !"

His hearer is quite incapable of having her thoughts conducted into the cheerfuller channels he thus tries to lead them into. Her eyes are still flashing wetly, and her colour high.

" How dare he invent such calumnies ? What does he mean ? What motive can he have ?"

" Probably he believes them to be true ; sometimes "—with a dispirited gesture—" I am half of his way of thinking. Sometimes I agree with him that, as he tersely puts it, my old-world lumber ought to be cleared out of the way of the really good conscientious work of the young fellows ; it is surprisingly clever, some of it ; look at that, now !"—in a key of renewed alacrity and genuine interest, as he takes into his hand a little terra-cotta model of a Breton peasant, with her wooden shoe on the rocker of her infant's cradle—" that was brought me a week or two ago by a boy I sent to study in Paris last year ; is not it good ? Did you ever see the *ewig mutterliebe* more charmingly expressed ?"

" I do not see much in it," she answers pettishly, scarce deigning a look at the work of art indicated, while in her ears there ring, in dismal confirmation of the reviewer's venomed words, the phrases employed by her over-night companion on the Terrace of the House of Commons.

Coke had expected her to receive his suggestion of decadence with derisive laughter, and vehement disclaimers, and little as she either is, or pretends to be, of an art critic, her silence dashes him. To shake off the sense of oppression derived from her lugubrious air, he cries in a tone that only an ear to which the inflections of his voice are very familiar could detect to be not really mirthful :

" Perhaps he is a liar; perhaps he had a fit of indigestion while he was writing; perhaps my guilty conscience misleads me, and my Sheffield patron had never heard of him or his review ; anyhow, my dear friend " —with a tinge of exasperation, half, and only half, feigned—" if you go on looking at me with those tragic eyes, you will drive me to borrow some of my scissor-maker's cutlery to put an end to myself with."

" I know that my long face is very trying," she says, ashamed and remorseful. " But you have taken my breath away." A minute later, in a tone of brusque decision : " You must do something great—stop their mouths with something indisputable."

It is not till she reaches the end of this phrase that she recognises that it is a parrot repetition of the diplomat's over-night.

" Why should not it be the fountain ?"

" I have thrown up the commission. The old lady's views and mine differed too radically, so I bowed her out."

" Then you no longer wish for Pamela Capel-Smith as a sitter ?"

She speaks in a furtive voice, as one conscious that she is laying a trap. Into it —such is the duplicity of man—her friend falls—at least, to the extent of maintaining a misleading silence. He takes up a syringe, and begins to squirt at the wet-clothed bust without answering. She cannot resist the temptation of letting him know that she is better informed than he suspects.

" At least," she goes on, " it was not as a Nereid that you were trying to persuade her to pose for you, when you met her at ——."

He gives a perceptible start, and drops his squirt, turning round with a flushed face and a guilty laugh.

" You are a magician; there is no use trying to hide anything from you—not that I did try ; I do want to persuade her to sit to me. I did ask her, and got a 'No' like a box on the ear for my pains. I dare say "—with a touch of bitterness—"that one of these coming young Phidiases would have got a different answer."

" No, that I am sure he would not!"—stoutly.

" I wanted her to sit to me for Eos—yes, Aurora—only the Greek name is so much the more beautiful. I never saw a human being who was such a bodily presentment of morning ; of course "—regretfully—"one could not give in marble her look of dewy newness ; she should have been just stepping into her car. I have got a splendid horse for her coursers ; she should have been throwing a kind look over her shoulder back at poor old Tithonus."

Anne's throat is certainly a little dry this afternoon.

" And who sits for poor old Tithonus?"

" Oh, he is not there at all ; he is understood, not expressed. However"—with a vexed gesture, and a resumption of his syringing—" she would not, and there is an end on't. It is a pity, for I have a sort of instinct that it would have been the making of me !"

" That it would have been the making of you!" repeats Mrs. Bligh thoughtfully.

CHAPTER XIII.

Of the two engagements made by Mrs. Bligh on the evening of her return home, one yet remains to be fulfilled, the Happy Evening for Factory Girls in Poplar, and on the evening upon which it falls due she sets out with no particular elation of spirit to fulfil it. Whatever the evening may prove to the girls, she has not much expectation of its being a " happy evening " to her. Naturally a shy woman, her spirit during the tedious transit in the sordid District Railway is sinking ever lower and lower, and as the last but one of the smoke-grimed stations is reached and passed, she puts to her companion a faltering query as to the topics she had best choose, and the method to be adopted most calculated to draw out the unknown and dreaded objects of this her first spurt of philanthropy.

" I think you will find they do not need much *drawing out*," replies the other, laughing, with a dryness upon which Anne's after-experience throws a lurid light.

They have reached their destination : a large bare room, used indifferently for night-schools, committees, classes, and treats. It is aflare with gas, and resounding with riotous female merriment, of which two or three ladies, rendered helpless by the overwhelming majority opposed to them, are vainly trying to stem the tide. Mrs. Bligh is aware that it is to supply the place of one of the habitual workers in this loud field of labour that her amateur services have been asked. It now transpires that one or two more of the ordinary staff have failed to appear, so that it is with lamentably inadequate forces that the little army of civilization to-night takes the field. The girls are evidently aware of and exhilarated by this fact. They are rushing

round the room after one another in rude
horseplay, with facetious familiarity flinging
their arms round the visitors' waists, and
gripping their hands with fingers that would
have made pale the raven's wing. For a few
moments Mrs. Bligh stands bewildered and
deafened, then, pulling herself together, she
says to her introducer to the pandemonium,
raising her voice to something like a shout to
enable herself to be heard :

" Would it be possible to make them quieter
by reading to them ?"

The other shakes her head.

" Most of them would not be read to ; if
there were enough of us we might draw a
few of the quieter ones into a second room
and read to them, but the majority prefer
conversation."

" *Conversation !*" repeats Anne, with a
grimly ironical smile, as a fresh burst of
screeching laughter and a fresh steeplechase
over the benches make the very walls ring ;
" and I thought they wanted drawing out !"

" They are better than they were !" replies

the other apologetically. "One of them used to stand on her head!" And then she dives into the *mêlée*, followed—though without much idea of what she will do when she gets there—by Anne.

But the obstreperousness of the fifty or sixty half-savage girls, tied down all day to some sedentary occupation, and indemnifying themselves generously now for the self-restraint of their working-hours, has got to a point far beyond the very inadequate means of control at the disposal of the visitors. It is, if anything, risen to a higher storm-pitch than ever, when the drama takes a new development, through the arrival on the scene, by a door into an adjoining room in which— as it now appears—a missionary meeting is being held, of an irate and remonstrant curate.

"I must really beg you ladies to be so good as to make a little less noise. The Bishop of Mngundi is speaking, and it is impossible to hear a word he says. His lordship is giving some very interesting details

about the Mngundi Mission, which are entirely lost."

The reproof is, indeed, a just one ; and the
poor helpless ladies accept it with a meek-
ness that is almost tearful.

" It is most unfortunate ! There are so
few of us to-night, the girls seem to have got
quite out of hand. Oh, thank Heaven "—in
a new key of relief and hope —" here is Miss
Capel-Smith ! she is such a favourite with
them ! perhaps she will be able to do something with them."

Miss Capel - Smith ! Pamela ! With a
bewildered feeling that her ears—whose
drums might easily have given way under
the strain lately imposed upon them—must
be playing her false, Anne bends her look
in the direction whither, as she sees, most of
the touzled heads and beflowered hats are
now turning, and recognises indeed, in the
figure making its smiling, joking way among
them, her most unexpected young friend.
The good effect of her advent makes itself
almost instantaneously felt. The senseless

inarticulate noise—made merely for noise's
sake—which has hitherto prevailed, is exchanged for loud expressions of welcome;
and in the eagerness to hold her hand in their
dirty clasp, they discontinue their earlier
pastime of boxing and cuffing each other.
With an admiration which, however, does
not impart the power of imitation, Anne sees
the well-carried little high head turning this
way and that among the gigantic bangs; sees
the delicate hand surrendered, without the
faintest indication of wincing from the contact, to the embrace of fingers none the less
sticky for being extremely affectionate. She
has not even gloves on, and is in the act of
yielding up her rings with unforced cheerfulness for examination when Anne reaches her
side.

"Is Saul also among the prophets?" says
Mrs. Bligh, in a low voice, so as not to be
heard by the crowding girls, and raising her
eyebrows as she speaks.

"Anne!"

There is almost the old joy at the sight of

her friend, mixed with the extreme surprise
of Pamela's tone, almost and yet not quite.
It is as if a thin gauze were drawn over the
real pleasure of her tone.   Anne laughs.

"We are most unflatteringly astonished to
find each other in the pursuit of good works.
I thought you were in the country."

"So I am : I mean I came up only this
afternoon.   Do you think"—reproachfully—
"that, if I had been at home, I should not
have been on the doorstep of the dear little
house to welcome you ?"

Anne gives a sort of start.   The words are
identical with those used by the sculptor in
explaining his failure to visit her.   Neither
of them had come to welcome her, yet both
have employed the same almost exaggeratedly
affectionate phrase.   Once before, as she now
recalls, she had been made reasonlessly uncomfortable by a similar accidental identity
of expression between them.

"The dear little house and the dear little
doorstep are still there ; when will you come ?
I have something to say to you."

At the last clause of her speech a flash of what looks like alarm comes into the girl's eyes.

"No bad news? nothing—nothing about Anglesey?"

Again Anne laughs dryly.

"Poor Anglesey! No, Anglesey is as well as can be expected."

But at this point Miss Capel - Smith's attention is imperatively claimed by her young factory friends, who noisily demand the names and value of the stones in her rings; and until the "Happy Evening" is over, no further private talk is possible. But the humanizing influence of Pamela, aided by the other ladies, whom her opportune arrival and exertions have enabled to regain their breath and their wits, aided also to the best of her ignorant ability by Anne, enables the remainder of the "Recreation" to be passed in a more reasonable manner than at its pandemonic opening had seemed possible; and no further irruption of exasperated clergy from the meeting next door is necessary.

When the end has come, and the lady workers are hurrying to the District Railway station, whence they are to take their westward way to their distant homes, Mrs. Bligh again approaches Pamela.

" You will come to me to-morrow? At what hour? I really have something to say to you."

" I hope "- with a rather nervous inflection -" that it is something pleasant."

" H'm! *c'est selon;* 'what's one man's meat is another man's poison !'"

" That always sounds to me such a difficult proverb to pronounce," says Pamela giggling, not quite like herself; "there are so many S's in it !"

" But you *will* come ?"

" Of course I will; do I "—with a return to some of the old tender expansiveness of manner—"do I often need pressing when it is a question of enjoying your society? I will "—laughing naturally this time—" be on the dear doorstep while it is still being scoured !"

18

" That is all right ; I am so———"

But at this point Mrs. Bligh's speech breaks suddenly off, as she discovers, with an unavoidable shrinking from the contact, that one of the factory girls is with coarse friendliness thrusting her arm through hers. Several of them have insisted on escorting the ladies to the station. One has already tucked Anne's introducer under her arm ; and shouts out to a companion, *apropos* of Mrs. Bligh :

" There's a poor lidy with no one to look arter 'er !   Florry, you look arter 'er !"

Florry is not slow to comply, and screams back :

" I can't get 'old on 'er ; she's got a cloak on !   Ah !" — triumphantly — " I 'ave 'er now !"

*   *   *   *   *

Pamela is as good as her word. The doorstep is still in process of scouring next morning when she presents herself upon it. She is shown into the drawing-room, where Anne, with a basin by her side, is on her knees beside the most languishing of her sick palms, scrubbing it with soap and water. She kisses her visitor with a preoccupied air, and they both sit down and look at each other. Pamela is the first to break silence.

" I was so surprised to see you last night ! Of course I know how radically kind-hearted you are, but I did not think that Poplar was quite your line of country ! Did you take kindly to it ?"

Anne laughs.

" I sat one day at dinner by an Eton boy, and seeing him make wry faces over a glass of old port, I asked him whether he liked it. ' No,' he said : ' I hate it, but it makes one feel so jolly !' I live in hopes of my good works making me feel jolly in time "—in another key—"one must fill one's life with *something*, when it is so ludicrously empty as mine! but "—hurrying on as if to avert the compassion the last sentence might seem to ask for—" is not it a new departure for you, too ?"

" Perhaps my life also is empty," replies the girl, with a rather impatient accent,

"Well, no, not exactly empty, but"—looking embarrassed—"when I came back from Wales, I felt so upset and 'no how,' you understand, that I thought the best thing I could do was to take up some practical work."

"I am afraid the good of the factory girls was not the leading motive in either of our minds."

"No, and yet"—with a lovely light of compassion in her starry eyes—"I am dreadfully sorry for them; I *should* like to make their lives a little less hideous."

"Oh, poor devils! I am sorry enough for them too," replies Anne, in a tone which betrays a good deal of compunction at her own callousness. "But to tell the truth"— her incorrigible candour getting the upper hand again—"last night I was a good deal sorrier for myself."

The subject drops, and a silence which has more of the awkward in it than would seem likely in the case of intimacy such as theirs, supervenes. Anne has resumed her squatting attitude, and her sponging.

"I am afraid," begins Pamela, "that my time with you is limited, so if you have anything you wish to say to me——" She pauses, but the other is rubbing so vigorously that it would seem she did not hear. "Have you anything you wish to say to me, or did I misunderstand you last night?"

Mrs. Bligh drops her sponge with a flop into the china bowl beside her, and looks her interlocutor straight between her eyes.

"Why will not you sit to Sir Robert Coke?" she asks, shooting out her question with the suddenness, and almost the violence, of a projectile.

The thrust is so unexpected that its victim has no time to make ready weapons of defence, or in any way protect or hide the small face, which in an instant becomes a sheet of dazzling blushes.

"Has he told you, has he been—been complaining of me?"

"That is no answer to my question. No, of course he has not been complaining of you; it would not be the least like him"—

indignantly.—" he is far too chivalrous. I learnt it indirectly. But why will not you sit to him ?"

The tone in which this demand is made is so far more imperative than its utterer has any idea of, that Pamela laughs nervously.

"Is it Anne?" she asks, holding up her hands with a half-playful, half-frightened gesture of warding off a threatened attack, "or is it Queen Eleanor, with the dagger and the bowl?"

Mrs. Bligh has by this time risen to her feet, and is standing over her disciple, still unconsciously gripping her sooty sponge.

"It cannot be prudery," she says, as if addressing herself rather than the girl. "I have never seen the least trace in you of that contemptible quality; and, besides, there would be no place for it. You would have your stepmother, or your maid, or that old governess of yours—I can't remember her name—during the whole of your sittings."

"Yes, of course I might," nervously answering this assault.

" Perhaps you are afraid of the irksome-
ness and fatigue of having to keep in one
position for so long?" continues Anne, her
unconsciously commanding tone changing
into one of eager persuasion. " But he
would be *most* considerate to you ; he would
let you rest as often as you liked, and you
would have his conversation to distract you.
Many women "—with a gallantly swallowed
sigh—" admired women—women very much
in the world, would think it no great hard-
ship to have him to talk to them for an hour,
or a couple of hours at a time." There is
not even an indistinct murmur in answer this
time, only a dead silence. " You think that
you are doing a good work," continues the
other, her voice swelling with indignation
at the dumb resistance offered to her argu-
ments, " when you allow those factory girls
to drag you about, and claw you ; and you
do not seem to see how very much greater
an act of charity it would be to give essential
help at a critical moment—with so little cost
to yourself, too—to a man of real genius !"

Apparently her friend's attitude—standing in such heat of expostulation over her, and waving the soapy sponge above her head—is more than Pamela can bear, for she now springs up and betakes herself to the window, where she stands with her back to the room, and whence a sound of uncomfortable remonstrant laughter now makes itself heard.

" Dearest Anne, what gross exaggeration ! *Essential help.*"

" I suppose," resumes Anne, beginning to march about the lonely little room with her hand behind her, " that the same thing happens to almost every genuine artist. In most of their lives there comes a moment when the fire seems to burn low ; when the spring ceases to run ; a moment of exhaustion ; and then, unless some new inspiration comes, something to start them again, to give them a fresh fillip, a new lease of artistic life——"

"And is it possible that you mean to imply that *I* can do all this for him ?" The girl's voice is quivering, and the colour burns in two fixed blazing patches under her eyes, but she looks her companion full and directly in the face.

"I do not know whether you can, but I know that he thinks you can ; which comes to much the same thing. Oh, *do* consent!" dropping the unheeded sponge at last on the carpet, and gripping Pamela's wrists ; "or, if you will not, at least give a reason for your refusal ; any reason, even a bad one ; come, I will take even a bad one—a bad one!"

There is a pause. The elder woman's face, not quite unlovable in its expressive plainness, is dyed in a hue as deep though not as lovely as hers whom she so urgently apostrophizes.

"Is it possible," says the latter, bringing out the question with low-voiced difficulty, "that you *really* wish me to sit to him?"

Anne laughs rather harshly.

"It is a little late in the day to ask that! Do you suppose, then, that I have been *joking* all this time ? Do I look, do I sound as if I were in joke ? But come," giving the other's slender captive wrists an impatient jog, "your reason, if you have one, which I am beginning gravely to doubt?"

" My reason," repeats Pamela, turning her head from side to side, as if looking for some way of escape ; but finding none, pulls herself together, and says with a heavy sighing breath, in a hurried low voice, "since you will have my reason, it was that I—I—was *afraid.*"

" *Afraid !*   Afraid of what !"

" Of --of—myself !"

An oppressive silence of several moments, so oppressive that Pamela finds even explanatory speech preferable.

" I need not dilate to you, who know him so well, upon his attractiveness. If I sat to him I should have to see a great deal of him ; you know his caressing manner to women : it means nothing, less than nothing, but I was afraid of getting too much *sous le charme.*   I do not think I have a stronger brain than other girls, and I was afraid that I might—I might—lose my head !"

Her utterance is rapid and very low ; and here she stops, dropping her eyelids and blushing intolerably. Mrs. Bligh has let loose her hold upon her young friend's hands and stepped back a pace ; each of her dark eyes seems to have secreted a burning coal in its pupil. Pamela has told her the truth, but not the whole truth ; one, and the more important half of it, she has suppressed, out of regard to her friend's feelings. On the simple page of that fair and loyal face before her Mrs. Bligh reads the innocent secret, that what Pamela has feared more than the loss of her own heart, is the filching of that one which she has—alas ! so erroneously— believed to be, or at least have been, Anne's possession. The feelings awakened by this discovery are of too potent a nature to make utterance easy, or at first even possible. But by-and-by she manages—though she does not quite know how she gets hold of it—to speak in a respectably steady voice, and with a grave smile.

" I think you were still more afraid that

someone else might lose his head! But," she pauses for a second, then resumes still more steadily than before, "why should you be afraid of *that* ?"

"But I am not," cries poor Pamela, in an agonized voice, the carmine usually limited to lips and cheeks deluging every visible inch of her. "Do not for a moment suppose that I was implying anything so fatuous. I am speaking—thinking—only of myself. Do not, for heaven's sake, put such an interpretation on my words! It would be too—*too* —fatuous !"

She breaks off choked with maiden shame. Anne has in her turn fled to the window, and in feverish absence of mind tweaked off one of the blossoms from a sole and expensive pot of lilies of the valley. Then she comes back, puts her arms round Pamela, and kisses her almost solemnly.

"There is nothing fatuous in it," she says, in a tone of great kindness. "It is *most* probable, and—and—*most* to be desired !"

"Oh no, no !" with almost tearful em-

phasis ; " it is most *im*probable, and most to
be *un*desired ! He can't help saying pretty
graceful things to other women, but it is
you, *you*, who are his real object—his real
devotion."

Anne passes her hand over her forehead.
The words so sincerely meant sound with
a horrible irony in her ears.

" My dear child," she says, mastering herself with great difficulty, "you have said
those sort of things till you believe them.
Let me earnestly beg of you, once for all,
to credit me when I assure you upon my
honour that Sir Robert Coke and I are
friends and good comrades—nothing more!
What should we be more, indeed? I am
very proud "—almost loudly—"of being his
good comrade. We like each other as two
men might—two very nice men. He *is* a
very nice man, and "—smiling—" it is more
my misfortune than my fault that I am not
a very nice man too."

And thus it comes to pass that Miss Capel-
Smith consents to sit to Sir Robert Coke.

She does not stay long after her shy and remorseful consent has been wrung out of her; but short as the interval is, it seems long to Anne. The sort of awkwardness which, as both now realize, has been growing up between them ever since the sculptor's shadow fell upon their friendship, and which had melted under the fire of their joint excitement half an hour ago, settles down upon them again despite all their efforts. With a sigh of relief Anne hears the hall-door shut behind her guest. She is standing before the fire, and as her eyes meet her eyes in the Chippendale looking-glass, a grim smile breaks over her face, as with an expressive gesture, as of one who has cut her own throat, she passes her forefinger along its surface from ear to ear.

"It will be brought in *felo de se*," says she, speaking out aloud, according to her wont. Then she sits down upon the floor again, and finishes washing her palm.

CHAPTER XIV.

Anne Bligh loses no time in informing her sculptor of the good turn she has done him. The first draft of the note on which she does so runs thus:

"Dear Friend,

"Your Ewe has been brought to hear reason. You will find her now willing to throw a smile over her shoulder at old Tithonus.

"Your *Deus ex Machinâ*,

"A. Bligh."

She reads it over complacently at first, with less satisfaction a second time, then tears it up. "It is ungenerous to sneer at his age. He can no more help being fifty than I can help being unattractive." She takes another sheet.

"DEAR FRIEND,

"I have persuaded Miss Capel-Smith to sit to you. Will you communicate directly with her? I enclose her address, in case you have not got it.

"Yours ever,

"A. BLIGH."

Her pen has halted a little over the "Yours ever." It is his invariable signature to her, which she has, with hesitating pleasure, adopted. But would not it be well to alter it now? "It would be truer with an 'n' before it—'Yours never.'" Then she thinks of that of Mr. Moddle—"Unalterably, never yours, Augustus"—laughs out loud, and, with just a passing wish that she had never adopted it, lets the usual formula go.

For the next day or two she is the prey of a dread which sometimes wears the face of a hope that he will come and thank her in person. But he does not. He sends her his gratitude in a prompt and ecstatic note, in which he calls her his dear "little friend, and his good angel"—handsome expressions which scarcely fill her with the joy they would have done had they been spontaneous, and not the acknowledgment of the particular kind of service rendered by her. The billet contains also the expression of an eager wish to come and see her, and talk over things, as soon as he can find a moment's breathing-space.

But as the days go by it becomes evident that that breathing-space has not been, and probably will not be, reached. Her common-sense coming to her aid, she gives up hurrying home, breaking through every other engagement to be back at her own tea-table by five o'clock.

The private view - day of the Royal Academy, for which he has sent her tickets, has arrived, and she has neither seen nor heard anything further of Coke, or his intending model. Probably on that general

19

meeting-ground of the smart, the artistic, and the frumpy she will come across them both. But she comes across neither, for the excellent reason that neither is there. Is it, she asks herself—as she walks through the crowded rooms alone, for she has hampered herself with no companion—is it merely that shyness and dread of overheard comment and disparagement which keeps a good many sensitive artists away, or a consciousness that his work this year is not up to its usual mark, that is accountable for his absence ?

The sculpture-room is always empty, so that, as she tells herself, the fact that no one is looking at Coke's " Marsyas" when she nears it is no indication of unsuccess. She walks round the group, and with rather a sinking heart observes how insignificant is the flaw in the marble back—how inadequate an excuse for the purchaser's refusal to take it ! She is regarding it somewhat ruefully, when someone touches her on the arm, and looking round with a start, and with heaven knows what sudden expectation, she sees Lady St. George!

"How are you? I do not care about it, do you? There is something strained in the attitude; but between you and me, I cannot stand modern sculpture; only"—with a knowing nod—"I do not tell our friend so. But"—with animation—"do tell me where 1463 is? A bust—they are all so alike—and so hideous! But they tell me it is *the* thing to look at—quite a new man. Young, and was a stone-mason; picked up by the wife of the Squire of his parish; *quite* a working man. I have no doubt he puts his knife half-way down his throat—but I must get hold of him."

Mrs. Bligh helps her friend to find 1463; owns grudgingly that it is not bad for a beginner; and goes home in spirits that would be yet more dispirited than they are, were she not supported in some measure by the thought that by next year the effect of the new inspiration to which she herself has been the means of helping her sculptor will be triumphantly displayed to the world. And meanwhile reason tells her that she must construct her life without any reference to him.

It seems hard that the having done one of her two most intimate friends a service should have robbed her of both, but as the weeks slip by she has sardonically to allow to herself that something not unlike this paradoxical result has been attained.

Yet Coke does pay his promised visit after awhile; but as ill-luck would have it—*he* may call it good-luck is her after-reflection —one or two of her not very numerous acquaintances have chosen the same day and hour to visit her; and though, as he rises to take leave after half an hour of trivial general chat, she cannot keep out of her eyes an entreaty to him to outstay her other guests, he either does not see, or disregards the dumb request. All she learns from that tantalizing snatch of his company is that he is in admirable looks and spirits, and appears in no wise annoyed at his failure to secure a *tête-à-tête.*

As to Miss Capel-Smith, whose exaggerated estimate of herself, and insatiable thirst for her society, had till lately filled her with protesting wonder, it is but in snatches that she catches a glimpse of her also. She runs in now and again, but though extremely, and, as it strikes Anne, remorsefully affectionate in her manner, she is always in a hurry, and never quite at her ease. She does not volunteer, nor can Mrs. Bligh bring herself to ask any information as to the sittings which the elder woman knows to be now in full swing. Pamela has had no gout to get the better of; and she is nineteen instead of fifty, and yet, or the other fancies it, there is a near kinship between the thinly-veiled exuberance of life and joy in the more than mature man and the scarcely-ripe girl. "It is certainly coming," Anne says to herself with a dry sob, which makes Tory give a short bark of interest and surprise—"If I am not a perfect fool I shall get my life into some sort of shape before it comes."

Nor does the resolution end in words.

Day by day she tries more and more earnestly to give it effect in action, seeking with feverish eagerness to find channels into which to pour that energy of being and fulness of feeling for which she has now no natural outlets afforded. To the surprise of the acquaintance who had introduced her to that sphere of labour, and witnessed her excessive distaste for it, she asks to be allowed to repeat her visit to Poplar, and though she can never be said to become very fond of the factory girls, yet it grows with her into a habit to forego her dinner every Monday night in order to cut out skirts and jackets for those boisterous young operatives—a share of the work which she has asked for as being most within her powers—and to discover how unexpectedly particular and difficult to please they are as to the fit of those garments.

Nor does she confine herself to the factory hands. Charity organization lays a claw upon her. She dabbles in "friendly girls," and "lost mothers," and "cabmen." Nor is it philanthropy alone that absorbs her in her quest of an existence of many-sided interests. She attends three courses of lectures; she eagerly follows up any opening that may lead to a widening of her narrow social circle. In London, probably more than in any other capital, the golden rule of "cutlet for cutlet" holds sway; and as the last census revealed the inconvenient richness in womankind of the British Isles, represented by a surplus of nine hundred thousand fair ones, there is naturally no great demand for an undinner-giving, unillustrious, unbeautiful solitary woman. But she accepts the few enter-tainments that are offered to her; and, as she does her best to make herself pleasant at them, they lead to more. Thus the weeks pass, and the month of poetic name and associations — the month of cuckoo and nightingale; often, also, of bitter breath and pinching easterly airs; the month when the Derby is run; and the missionaries "from the plains of Timbuctoo" throng Exeter Hall; and the lilac has its brief span of exquisite life—draws to a close.

Mrs. Bligh has not yet reached that stage
of existence when life goes by electric tele-
graph.   At twenty-nine it has not more than
the speed of the Flying Dutchman ; and of
late it has been going more slowly than
usual through being so much more and
more variously filled.   Much slower, for
instance, than during the last three un-
eventful weeks of her visit to the Mulhollands.

The Mulhollands! How little they have
been in her thoughts of late is brought home
to her when, on letting herself into her house
one afternoon, she finds her parlour - maid
spelling out the florid message of regret at
having missed her, scratched on a card left a
few minutes before by Czar.

He is up then, embarked on his career of
pleasure, in his comfortable bachelor rooms ;
and having left his long - suffering family
behind him with as little compunction as he
had left the spring cabbages and peas in his
garden.   Her indignation at his selfishness
prevents her from taking any notice either

of him or his pencilled despair. In a few more days he has passed utterly out of her head.

One morning early in June she is at her bureau, puzzling over the accounts of a charitable society which she has undertaken to keep in order during the absence, through illness, of its secretary. The pugs are sitting in the window, with their backs turned to her, looking like a couple of Morland's pigs. Tory is sitting upright, as a sort of protest against her mistress's absolute refusal to saddle herself with her weight upon her lap. Sall is occasionally trying with hand and mouth to catch a torpid blue-bottle on the pane. Both are bored and *désœuvré*. But all of a sudden they spring to their feet, breaking into a storm of barks, which are taken up and answered by other dog-voices from below.

Mrs. Bligh asks them to stop, but since they pay no attention, being as disobedient as women's dogs always are, she puts her fingers resignedly in her ears, and goes on counting. But after the lapse of a minute or two, she becomes aware that the door has opened, and visitors, whose names, thanks to her stopped ears, she has not caught, are being announced.

Who can be sufficiently intimate with her to call upon her at eleven in the morning? She is not long left in doubt.

"I do not know what you will say to our bringing the dogs!" says Mrs. Mulholland, appearing in the doorway, followed by her daughter and stepdaughter, the former bearing her beloved Fezy, in a state of overpowering agitation at the sight of the pugs, and the latter leading Jim in a string; "but we did not dare to leave them at the hotel; they have got us into sad hot-water already!"

"Jim would not have thought of biting that idiot of a waiter if he had sat down at once," cries Lucile indignantly. "You remember he never can bear to see anyone that he does not know, standing up; if he had sat down at once——"

"I am afraid"—in laughing interruption—

"that waiters, as a rule, cannot do much sitting down!"

"And I dare say the invalid lady whom Fezy kept awake all night with his barking is not much of an invalid really," cries Sue warmly; "and if they send him downstairs to sleep in the kitchen to-night, they shall send me too! We will be found dead in each other's arms among the blackbeetles!"

They all laugh.

"He had better take a bed here; "I wish"—hospitably—"you could all take beds here! I had not an idea that you were up. I was out when Czar called."

"I think," says Mrs. Mulholland, with a mildly reproachful tinge in her good-natured voice, "that he was a little bit piqued at your taking no notice of his card. His lady friends, as a rule, are so very *empressé*. He is too proud to say so; but I think he rather expected you to ask him to have a cup of tea, or——"

Anne feels herself growing guiltily pink.

"I should not have ventured to invite

such a swell! I know he is always so over-
whelmed with engagements."

Czar's wife hesitates.

"He has not quite so many invitations
this year as he expect—as usual; his friends
do not seem to be giving much; they are all
very smart people, and have shut up their
houses on account of the royal mourning!"

Anne struggles with a smile at the
ingenuity that has evidently been needed
by the old gentleman in reconciling the discrepancy between his rose-coloured accounts
of his own popularity and the actual fact.

"And so he brought you all up to console
him!"

Again Mrs. Mulholland hesitates, and
there is evidently a slight struggle in her
mind before she replies.

"Well, no, he did not bring us up, much
as he would have liked it; the fact is, we are
up for a week on the strength of a cheque
sent me by an eccentric old cousin of Czar's,
with the stipulation that it should be spent
entirely on a treat for me and the children!

Of course, one must not look a gift-horse in the mouth ; but we were all a little indignant at her excluding poor Czar so pointedly. However, he took it very sweetly, and begged us to enjoy ourselves."

" There is very little doubt "—smiling openly this time—" about your being able to oblige him in that particular !"

" Oh no, of course not ; only "—with a rather harassed look—" unfortunately we all want to go different ways. Lucile to South Kensington and the Military Tournament ; Sue to Westminster Abbey and the Dogs' Home ; and I to the Stores, and "—with a rueful glance at Jim and Fezy, to whom the pugs are making advances of mixed ire and coquetry—" there are so few places where dogs are admitted."

" London is not a nice place for dogs ; I " —doubtfully—" am a little surprised at your bringing them up."

" Well, you see, Sue never will be separated from Fezy."

" He would break his heart if I were to

desert him," cries the little girl, interrupting her darling in the marked homage he is paying to Tory by snatching him up in her arms, "and then I should break *my* heart, and we should be buried in one grave !"

"And we would put over you, ' They were noisy and unpleasant in their lives,' " etc., interjects Lucile, laughing.

Anne laughs too.

"Fezy, I own, is accounted for ; but why Jim ?"

"George asked us to bring him up to meet him."

"George is in London too ?"

"Yes, he is on his way to his new agency, buying things for his house."

"His agency ? His house ?" in a tone of surprised interest.

"Oh yes, I was forgetting ; you have not heard our great news. George has got a land agency ; it appears that he is a wonderful judge of timber, which seems to be a thing that is born with you, and that you cannot acquire ; and on the strength of that and his being so good at accounts, Mr. Blank——"

" The nice man who brought us down from the slate-quarries on his engine "—puts in Sue explanatorily—"has got him a sub-agency. Poor fellow, we are all so glad for him."

" And so am I, heartily."

" As his chief lives on another estate, he is to have his house ; a capital house I am told, almost too good "—with a meaning look— " for a lonely bachelor."

That meaning smile, reflected in the girls' faces, tells Mrs. Bligh that hope of the attainment of their Blue Rose has revived in the minds of the Mulholland family—that Blue Rose which her own late action has made it more out of the question than ever for them to pluck. The consciousness of this fact makes her feel at once so shabby and so regretful, that she finds no words with which to hint to them that their castle is built on the sand ; and Mrs. Mulholland resumes in a contented voice :

" He is in great spirits, poor boy! He is coming to tell you himself; he always fancied that you did not think him good for much, so it is quite a little triumph for him. Do not let him know that we have been beforehand with him. Be very much surprised. Ah! here he is!" as the sound of the front-door bell is heard once again, moving the ire of the parlour - maid with its electric tremor, unwonted and unreckoned for in the fore-noon.

" I do not know whether I can manage being surprised; but I shall not have the slightest difficulty in being pleased," rejoins Anne, turning a face, dressed out in compunctious congratulations, towards the door, to be ready to greet the expected arrival.

But if Mrs. Bligh's congratulations are needed, they will have to be new-shaped to fit the requirements of a different object from the one looked for. George Mulholland would not bound into the room unannounced, in a hat wreathed with roses; nor pull himself up dead short in the middle of the room, with a little "Oh!" of consternation, at the sight of his mother and sisters.

The first glance at Pamela Capel-Smith's face tells Anne that she has come to make that announcement, which, as Mrs. Bligh has daily and hourly told herself, can have no element of surprise, much less shock, for her when it comes; since there is no moment of her waking hours in which she does not expect it. She is the one of the awkwardly silent group who pales instead of reddening.

"I did not know. I had not an idea," stammers Pamela, recovering her speech first, but imperfectly.

"We are such country cousins, that everybody is astonished to see us in London," says Mrs. Mulholland, with an air of stiff dignity which sits oddly on her; "but I do not see why we should not have our fling as well as our neighbours! We have paid you a visitation"—turning to Anne, and beginning to refasten the lace cloak — an obvious fruit of the cousin's legacy, which in the warm room she has let drop upon her ample shoulders. " Lucile, put Jim's muzzle on again."

" Jim," repeats Pamela, in a rather moved voice ; " is Jim here too ?"

Then, as he is drawn forth from beneath the sofa to which he has retired to avoid the hoydenish overtures of Sall and Tory, she puts out her hand to stroke him ; but some inward emotion makes her change her intention, and she contents herself with saying gently :

" Poor dear Jim ! he does not look much like a London dog."

" He does. not wish to !" cries Lucile— inducting, as she speaks, his reluctant pink nose and blinking eyes into their horrid little leather cage—"he would not if he could ; he hates London."

" We have brought him up to meet George! He is to live with George at his agency. George has got an agency," explains Sue eagerly, mentioning the name and giving the information which her elders have wished, but felt their perfect inability to introduce and impart. They glance gratefully at her.

"George has got an agency!" repeats Pamela, in a tone of lively interest, not unmixed with astonishment. "Oh!"—turning towards George's relatives with a sort of diffidence as to the manner in which her congratulations may be received—"I am so glad."

"We are all glad," replies Mrs. Mulholland, still stiffly, but with indications of a temptation to thaw; "he most of all. It was never his wish to be idle. Come, girls, are you ready?"

They file out: women, child, dogs, bidding a formal adieu to Miss Capel-Smith as they pass her; a formal one, all but Sue, who, yielding to the instincts of an ineradicably kind heart, and thinking that the culprit looks snubbed, insists on both Jim and Fezy shaking hands cordially with her. Anne accompanies her visitors to the hall-door, partly to do them honour, partly also from an unavowed wish to defer for yet a few moments longer the reception of those tidings which she knows that Pamela is feverishly waiting to impart.

But the adieux of the hurried little party, hastening to begin the cramming of a season's enjoyment into their one brief week, cannot be prolonged beyond two or three minutes, and however slowly she may mount her stairs, she gets back to the drawing-room before she can find any confidence that her armour against the coming blow is half braced on. She finds Miss Capel-Smith standing in the middle of the room evidently.in too great a tremor of nerves to sit down. The moment that her hostess appears she breaks out into eager speech.

"Never, *never* will I burst in upon you unannounced again! I would have given anything not to have met them here to-day!"

"It was unlucky."

"How cold they were to me—all but Sue. Dear little Sue! What a beautiful nature that child has!"

It is obvious to Mrs. Bligh that she is not

alone in her desire to put off the crucial moment. Pamela is evidently trying to shirk it too. But since it must come, it had better come at once.

"You did not"—with a strained smile—" come here to talk to me about Sue ?"

" Did not I ?"

" You have something more interesting to say ?"

" Have I ?"

The girl has turned her back to her friend, in obedience as the friend finds to that elementary law of humanity which teaches you, when you are thrusting five inches of cold steel into the heart or vanity of a fellow-creature, not to look at him or her while you are doing it.

" I am a true prophet, then ? It is settled?"

Mrs. Bligh's stairs are short and easy. It cannot be the climbing them that has made her so ridiculously short of breath. Pamela is stooping over Mrs. Bligh's modestly furnished silver table, fidgetingly handling the little objects upon it.

"It is all your doing!" she says in an agitated, low voice. "I owe it all to you! You first suggested the idea! But for you such a thought would never have crossed my brain."

All her doing. The listener neither accepts nor disclaims the imputed glory. She is realizing what a large difference there is between having the sword hung at ever so small a distance above your head, and the same sword actually slicing the tendons and arteries of your neck.

"Do you remember that day in Beaumaris Castle, when you snatched the lots out of my hand?"—not looking up, and speaking very quickly.

"Yes, I remember. I am so likely to forget"—aside.

"You said that I was *meat for George's masters!* It came upon me with a flash that you might mean *him.* Did you?"—with a ring of anxiety in her voice—"I am almost sure that you did."

"Yes, I meant *him.*"

Mrs. Bligh will be able, so she tells herself, to manage something more than these stupid assents in a moment or two.

" But it was only a flash," continues the other, "and it passed in a second ; in fact, I was deadly ashamed of its ever having crossed my mind."

" Yes ?"

" And then a little later on we stayed in the same country house for a Sunday, and he seemed to make a good deal of me, but I tried to think it meant nothing ! You see " —a slight pause—" I had got a stupid mistaken idea in my head, built upon nothing but my own silly fancies——"

She breaks off, and though Mrs. Bligh knows that the labouring sentence's drift is to try and convince her that her own conduct has given no colour to the silly fancies alluded to, she can still bring out nothing but another difficult " Yes ?"

" I was so afraid of giving way to my—my feeling for him, that I made up my mind I would avoid every chance of meeting him ;

and then I saw you at Poplar, and you told me to come and see you, and as, no doubt, you remember, you asked me to sit to him— begged it of me as a personal favour to yourself; that was what decided me, and since then" —her lovely face drooping rosily lower—" it has all been plain-sailing, and yesterday——"

" Only yesterday ?"

" Last night ; do you think "—enthusiastically—" that I should be likely to delay in telling *you—you* to whom I owe him ? Yes " —with moistening eyes and unsteady voice —" we both feel that you have given us to each other."

Mrs. Bligh breaks into what may pass muster for a laugh.

" I always knew that I was of a very generous turn !" Then, with a sudden change of key, " you are a foolish child, and you put it rather too strongly ; but I have —yes, I have "—her voice gaining in firmness—" tried to be a friend to you—*both.*"

" There never was such a friend !" cries the excited girl, half crying. " *He* says so ;

he says that if anyone you loved committed a murder, you would hide him under your bed! He says that the phrase 'True as steel' must have been made expressly for you. He says ——"

A sort of shiver passes over Anne. These phrases of repeated encomium are almost intolerably painful to her. To stem them, she says abruptly :

"And you—you now feel that 'something headlong,' as you called it, which you lacked before, and which poor George, with the best intentions in the world, was quite unable to inspire!"

A tiny cloud just skims over Pamela's radiant brow.

"I do not know what I feel—I am all in a whirl! Sometimes the honour and the responsibility seem almost more than I can bear! Never—*never* would such a presumptuous idea have entered my head if you had not put it there; you dear, *dear* Anne!"— throwing herself into her friend's arms—"it is *all* your doing!"

CHAPTER XV.

MISS CAPEL - SMITH'S expansive outbreak
precedes, by a very few minutes, her departure. When she is gone—her hostess accompanies her also to the hall-door—that hostess
stands before the empty fireplace, and looks
into the depths of that chimney-glass, to
which, in her solitary life, she has acquired
the habit of making confidences. "You
dear, *dear* Anne!" she says out loud, in a
mocking voice to the image which the mirror
gives her back; "it is all your doing!" and
repeating again more slowly: "You dear,
dear Anne, what an astonishing fool you
have been!" she drops into an arm-chair,
and, though the accounts of the charitable

society still remain unravelled out on her bureau, lies limp and idle for awhile.

Not a long while, however, since her morning's trials are not yet over. It is not much past noon when the door-bell sounds yet a third time, and she has only just succeeded in getting her countenance into some sort of order—not, indeed, that she has any tear-traces to remove—when " Mr. George Mulholland " is announced. During the last half-hour her pity for him has been wholly submerged in her warm compassion for herself, but it revives with a stab when she sees how indescribably smartened up and brightened he looks, how good a frock-coat he wears—the cousin's legacy again, doubtless and with how alert and hopeful an air, and how little of the clodpole, he enters. As he shakes her hand his eye wanders beyond her, evidently in search of some expected and not found object.

" I—I met my people just now," he begins ; " they told me that that——"

" That I should be delighted to see you !"

replies Anne hastily, finishing his sentence
for him in a way which, as she is well aware,
is not the one that he intended. His eye,
growing disappointed, still rambles. He
had, it is plain, hoped to find Pamela still
here. Is it as a propitiatory offering for
her that he has brought the magnificent
bunch of Marshal Niel roses which occupy
his left hand ?

"What superb roses!" she says, for the
sake of saying something, after they are both
seated.

" Do you like them ?" he answers, holding
them out rather diffidently to her. " I
thought that perhaps you might. I remem-
bered how fond of flowers you were at Plas
Drow."

They were not meant for Pamela, then.
He has bought them expressly for her, out
of the legacy, too, probably ! Is there no
way of stopping him from making these
repeated coal fires on the top of her guilty
head ? And what a return she has to make
to him ! These thoughts are working such

havoc in her mind and manners that she
entirely forgets to put out an answering hand
to receive the offered nosegay. Instead of
taking it, she cries out, to the surprise and
consternation of the would-be donor :

"Oh, but this is really too dreadful!"
Then, seeing the dismayed astonishment in
the young man's face, at this extraordinary
mode of reception, she recollects herself,
and stammers awkwardly : "I believe that
I am getting *Aphasia ;* is not Aphasia the
saying the exact opposite of what you in-
tend ? Of course, I mean how beautiful, how
delightful!"

But George is naturally not deceived by
this extremely lame explanation.

"Why should there be anything dreadful
in my giving you a few roses ?" he asks,
with a troubled voice, in which there seems
to be a sort of forecast of misfortune. "Is
it—have you" bringing out the words at
first stammeringly, and then with a blurt
"is it that you have been doing me any
more ill-turns ?"

His words make certain what she has all
along suspected—that he is aware of the
part she has had in his disaster, nor does
she in any way try to rebut the accusation.
She lays down the Marshal Niels, whose
cool stalks seem to burn her palm. She
cannot tell him while holding his flowers in
her hand. Obeying the humane rule lately
put in practice by Pamela for her benefit,
Mrs. Bligh keeps her eyes averted while she
deals her blow.

" It is too late ; it is out of my power now
for me to do you either a good or an ill turn !"

" What do you mean ?" hurriedly.

" I mean," still looking away, and almost
running her words into each other in her
eagerness to get the communication over,
"that the reason why Pamela came here
this morning was to announce her engagement to Sir Robert Coke !"

She ends, and still with lowered eyes waits
with lips compressed as if to bear an expected
prick of pain for the words of disappointment
and bitter sorrow which will surely follow.

But none such, not even an inarticulate
ejaculation, come. He is taking his punishment silently, as a man should. She steals
an anxious glance in his direction. He is
standing in exactly the same attitude as
when first he had entered the room, but
the whole look of brightness and smartness
has disappeared. Even his frock-coat seems
to have collapsed. Since she is looking at
him, it is evident that he thinks she is
expecting him to say something, so after an
obvious struggle he speaks :

" It was always your plan ; of course, you
are glad."

She winces. Is this his revenge—this
ironical assertion of her joy in her successful
labours? But a second glance at his face
assures her that he has had no such ironical
intention, that the speech is uttered in all
good faith, and that he is much too smothered
and swallowed up in his own woe to have
the most distant suspicion of hers.

" I—I thought it better you should know
at once," she murmurs miserably.

"Thank you; yes, of course—certainly—
it is better!"

He moves as he speaks, and, turning,
seems to be searching for his hat, with a
gesture as of one who does not see very well.
She divines what it is that has for the
moment obscured his strong young sight,
divines also his anxiety that she should not
guess the cause. She helps him to look for
his hat, and in a moment or two it is found.
Holding it in one hand, he offers her the
other.

"I am no worse off than I was before!"
he says, with a gallant attempt at a smile.
"One cannot lose what one never possessed."

The mixed self-respect and magnanimity
which, as she feels, have dictated this speech
are more than she can bear.

"It was inexcusable in me to meddle!"
she cries, in an irrepressible outbreak of
remorse. "It is too late now, and I dare
say you will not believe me; but if you knew
how deeply, *deeply* I regret——"

"You need not," he answers, with more dignity than she could have thought him capable of. "I think better of her than to believe that, if she had had one spark of real liking for me, she could have been turned against me by a comparative stranger after all these years!"

The succession of strong emotions—all disagreeable—which Mrs. Bligh has experienced during the brief compass of one forenoon produces in her the not unnatural result of a bad headache. It is not bad enough to justify taking it to bed, but is yet by dinner-time bad enough to make the thoughts of an evening party to which she is engaged particularly irksome. Were the party in question given by a prosperous member of society, she would not hesitate to refuse it the insignificant boon of her company. But as on the contrary it is the struggling effort at festivity of the wife of a far from successful artist, who had invited her *vivâ voce*, and with a profusion of apologies for the humility of the entertainment, her kind heart forbids her to yield to her ardent desire to shirk it.

To set off to an evening party, when you have not preceded it by dining out, always needs an exertion. The cold-blooded dressing after dinner, at an hour when nature bids you put off your artificial weeds, instead of enduing them, becomes yet more trying when you face it alone. It is therefore with a very jaded feeling of deep self-pity that Anne steps into her hired brougham, and joggles off to Metheglin Road in Kensington beyond Jordan. She finds the studio in which the entertainment is chiefly taking place so full of people that she regrets her unneeded philanthropy.

They are very odd-looking people—shaggy men, and queerly bedizened ill-combed women. As she recognises no acquaintances among them, she employs herself in looking at the pictures, of which the *atelier* contains a painful plenty. She knows that three or four have been refused by the Academy, and is reflecting how very little worse they are

than some of the triumphant daubs she has
lately seen hanging on the line at Burlington
House, when an affected and familiar voice
sounds in her ear.

" *Que diable*, Mrs. Nan, *va-t'elle faire dans
cette galère ?*"

She turns round with a start, but recovering herself, retorts with a smile :

" *Que diable*, M. Czar, *va-t'il faire dans
cette galère ?*"

"You may well ask !"—with a shrug.
"You do not suppose"—in anxious haste
to explain away his appearance in Metheglin
Road—"that I am often to be caught among
such a set of ragamuffins ; but one does a
thing of the kind, once in a ' blue moon,' for
a lark ! Though you would not believe it"
—laughing—" I have a strong streak of the
Bohemian in me, and one likes to be kind."

" Yes."

" But now that we have found one another
—ah, here are a couple of chairs—we can be
independent of all these unclean beasts !
Do you know, Mrs. Nan, that I have a crow

to pluck with you? Are you one of those ladies who never look at your cards, or are you aware that a poor old fellow came begging a cup of tea from you one sultry afternoon, and was turned broken-hearted from your door?"

"I was out," replies she briefly, the old temptation to stem the tide of his flummery coming back strongly upon her. "I am so glad"—speaking rather stiffly—"that you are all up this year, and gladder still about George's agency. I stupidly forgot to ask when and where it is."

"It is one of Lord ——'s," replies the old gentleman, his own voice stiffened by the perception of the little appetite shown by Mrs. Nan for his gallant reproaches.

"Lord ——!" repeats Anne, in a tone of surprise.

The title is that of the owner of the country house at which Pamela and her present *fiancé* had spent the delicious Sunday that had so potently influenced their after-destiny.

"Yes, Lord ——; do you know him?

He is a very old crony of mine ; we matriculated at Christ Church together. If you meet him—well "—chuckling—" I can only hope he will not tell tales out of school."

" I have no acquaintance with him."

" I suppose "—still chuckling—"that he expects to find George a chip of the old block. He will not be long in finding out his mistake ; poor George !"

" Poor George !" echoes Mrs. Bligh in a tone of such heart-felt compassion as at once procures her pardon for any previous omissions from her old companion, who naturally thinks that she is pitying his son for being so unlike his brilliant sire.

" He does not favour me much, as the servants say," continues George's parent complacently. " But he is a very good fellow in his way—a very good fellow indeed ! never given me an hour's anxiety. I am afraid "—with a look and smile of self-congratulatory reminiscence—" that my poor father would have had a very different story to tell when *I* was his age."

Mrs. Bligh's face does not reflect, even faintly, her companion's simper. She has none of her Plas Drow reasons for keeping him in good humour, and sees plainly that the tide of his reminiscences is bearing them both directly to the too-well-known tale of the four-wheeler and the injured husband.

"I think," she says, with a gravely determined effort to kill two birds with one stone —snub his father, and do George a tardy justice—"that the more one knows of your son, the more——"

Her sentence stops short, like a broken bridge in mid-air, for while it is still un-finished, her eye, straying carelessly round merely to avoid fixing itself on the grimacing old face beside her, sees by a stir near the door, and a thickening of the little crowd in that direction, that an arrival of more im-portance than any that have yet taken place is happening. Out of the clustering knot she presently sees emerge a figure whose air of distinction, heightened in this case by contrast, makes her break into a smile of

indignant incredulity, his own joking doubt
as to his ever having had a grandfather. He
is shaking hands cordially with half a dozen of
the dingy men and women, when Czar, dis-
covering the cause of Anne's sudden in-
attention to himself, cries :

" Why, bless me, here is our friend who
makes faces and busts ; our poor Coke !"

It has always seemed to comfort Czar for
the inequality between the sculptor's social
success and his own opinion of his merits, to
repeat frequently the flat old joke at his
expense, and prefix every mention of him
by the epithet—"poor." " Our poor Coke !"

To-night the epithet seems ludicrously
inapt. With his well-cut clothes, and his
Malmaison carnation, and his brilliant smile,
he seems to have as little relation as possible
with Czar's depressed and sordid adjective.

" Our poor Coke does not look very poor
to-night," she says dryly, and at the same
instant he catches sight of her.

In a second a sort of a cloud has come
over the radiance of his face, and he half

turns as if to move farther off. Good
heavens! how she must have given herself
away, when he, the least coxcombical of men,
is obviously afraid to meet her—to see the
havoc wrought in her by the sight of his new
bliss! She cannot, must not leave him for
an instant the prey of so humiliating a delusion. Without the slightest compunction she
quits Czar, and going up straight to Coke,
accosts him brusquely.

"I thought you never went to evening
parties."

"The exception proves the rule"—still
with that shade of embarrassment over his
whole person. "He is a dear old friend of
mine; we were in Paris together, as penni-
less art students, and lived in the Quartier
des Étudiants .for sixty francs a month each,
and dined when we could afford it at a jolly
dingy restaurant for eighteen sous, *pain à dis-
crétion;* afterwards our paths diverged——"

"As widely as Pharaoh's butler and
baker," interrupts she, with what she feels
to be an overdone air of ease and good

spirits. "You give the cup into Pharaoh's hand at Marlborough House, and he is hanged, or rather his pictures are not. But"—with a still more forced sprightliness—"you will have to give up Bohemia now. I do not quite see Pamela among these 'bangs and beads.'"

He looks at her, not very comfortably.

"Yes," he answers gravely. "I shall have to give up Bohemia." And she could almost fancy that there is a slight touch of regret in his voice.

They have passed out of the studio into a small adjoining room, where for the moment they are alone.

"I suppose," he says, with an almost shy smile, "that you are thinking that there is no fool like an old fool!"

Now is her moment, and she rushes upon it.

"On the contrary," she cries, with precipitate eagerness, lifting her moved lit face to his, "I think that you would have been the base Indian over again if you had not

snatched at the fine pearl that heaven threw
in your path."

"Rather that *you* threw in my path," he
answers, in a tone of emotion, too poignant
to be wholly pleasurable. "Dear, dear
friend, do you suppose that without your
sweet encouragement I should ever have
dared to match my November afternoon
with that exquisite April morning? You
know, as well as I do, that it is all your
doing."

She stoops her head in bitter acquiescence
with this second testimony to her own gift
for suicide.

"It is a tremendous venture," he goes on,
passing his hand through that hair, which,
though thick and wavy, yet shows un-
deniably the gray ensign of declining life.
"If it answers—if it answers "—repeating
the doubtful phrase with an energy of
anxiety that for the moment makes him
look old and worn—"the credit of it will
be all— *all* yours !"

    *   *   *   *   *

On the next day Mrs. Bligh has the pleasing task of imparting to the Mulholland family the downfall of their revived hopes, which George has—probably because he felt that their commiseration is more than he can bear—omitted to do. Their laments are loud and long.

"Why, he is old enough to be her grandfather!" cries Lucile indignantly; "there must be forty years between them."

"I cannot say much about that," says Mrs. Mulholland emphatically; "nobody has better reason than I to know how absolutely unimportant a discrepancy mere age is!"

"Then it was not a joke, after all, about his coming all the way to Plas Drow to see her?" is Sue's contribution.

"We all thought he was your property, Nan—did not we, girls?" from Mrs. Mulholland.

"I am sure that I never did or said anything to confirm so insane a delusion," replies "Nan," with an energy whose unnecessary bitterness she feels the moment it is too late.

"I am so sorry that I made Jim and Fezy shake hands with her!" almost sobs Sue. "Jim! Fezy!"—impressively taking hold of a paw of each—"you are never, *never* to shake hands with that lady again."

And then happily a hotel waiter enters and announces the arrival of a "young lady" from Russell and Allen, and a "young gentleman" from Peter Jones, with their respective parcels, and in the frenzied skurry of their London week, the subject of George's wrongs is happily shorn of some of the gigantic proportions it would have assumed in the quiet and leisure of Wales.

Mrs. Bligh does her duty thoroughly and warmly by her country friends, lunching, teaing, and dining them as often as she can prevail upon their delicacy to husband the rapidly dwindling legacy by sharing her roast mutton and bread-and-butter. She chaperones the girls untiringly to sights, and makes up Mrs. Mulholland's endlessly vacillating mind for her at every counter in London. She would always have rendered them these services out of gratitude and goodwill, but usually she would have thought them a *corvée*—now she is thankful for them, looking on the unbroken succession of tiresome little calls upon her time and attention as so many allies to keep thought at bay.

When the Mulhollands are gone, she throws herself with passion into her good works. In a moment of wild philanthropy she treats eleven of the Poplar factory girls to an afternoon at the Naval Exhibition; but after some hours of fervid heat and acute mental and bodily strain, returns home late in the evening a good deal crestfallen, with only seven of her *protégés* remaining; the other four having left her society for that of as many soldiers from Chelsea Barracks, whose appearance and manners pleased them, and from under whose martial care they mock her when she pursues them to the Cockpit of the " Victory " with kissed hands and farewell smiles.

The two people who have with such enthusiastic gratitude attributed their happiness to Mrs. Bligh do not, as the weeks go on, thrust that happiness upon her, nor does she, it is needless to say, intrude herself upon their new bliss. She has done them her good turn, and there is for the present nothing for her to do but quietly to efface herself from their orbit. She calls now and then on Pamela to avoid any appearance of coldness, but she usually chooses an hour at which she is likely to be out, and with the sculptor her intercourse is quite in abeyance.

Yet though she scarcely or ever comes across this pair of lovers of her own making, the consciousness that every hansom that flashes past *may* show them to her enclosed within the intimate precincts of its wooden flaps, that every walk she takes with the dogs in Kensington Gardens *may* reveal them pacing or sitting in dual felicity beneath the summer trees, keeps her feverish. She is far too sound and strong to fall ill, but she grows thin, and sleeps brokenly. When it is once irrevocable

—when they are one flesh—she will, so she tells herself, easily regain her equable spirits.

The marriage will certainly take place soon ; what is there for them to wait for ? and once in the list of accomplished facts, she has surely sense and strength of character enough to accept it peaceably. But though she longs with restless eagerness to learn the date of the intended union, from neither of the betrothed pair does she hear a word of tiding concerning it. And meanwhile, like Ritter Toggerburg,

"Ruhe Kann *sie* nicht erjagen."

One morning, after a more than usually unsatisfactory night, the question occurs to her, why she should put herself to the needless pain of this perpetual condition of dreading expectation. What is there to hinder her from going away, out of reach of the possibility of meeting those whom it is now her highest wisdom to avoid, and not returning until after they are wedded man and wife ? Why should not she go abroad ?

She had spent the first year of her widowhood on the Continent, so has gained the habit of solitary travel. Why should not she revisit those places where she had passed the first stupefied months of her release from her eight years' bondage, so that she may convince herself that, evil as her case now seems to herself, it is yet conspicuously better than when her stunned and dazed eyes had last rested on Leman's Lake or Chamouni's Glaciers ?

The plan approves itself so instantly to her mind that, within a fortnight of its first conception, she is making arrangements for the temporary devolvement of her philanthropical labours upon a fellow-worker; has presented herself at Mr. Cook's office ; is putting away her best china, and, most difficult task of all, is planting out the three dogs in homes where their frailties will be leniently dealt with. She has written to Pamela to inform her of her imminent departure, and has had a somewhat painful and unsatisfactory farewell visit from her ; painful from the girl's evident inability to conceal her remorseful conviction of the cause of her friend's oldened and altered looks, and premature departure, and unsatisfactory, because Pamela tells her nothing of her future plans. Perhaps, as Anne bitterly thinks, she supposes her unable to bear the hearing of them.

The visit has taken place in the morning, and in the late afternoon, when she has just thrown herself, tired and heated with final packings and puttings away, into her arm-chair, another caller is announced, whose name—thanks to the dogs being already removed to their temporary homes—she is actually able to catch.

"Sir Robert Coke!" She has not seen him, except in passing snatches, for over a month. Is it her sick fancy, or does he, despite his gray frockcoat and his Malmaison, look a degree or two less radiant than he did at his old Quartier Latin friend's shabby evening party? And if he does, is she mean enough to be glad of it?

"So you are going to leave us?" he says, complying with her request to sit down, but not choosing his once favourite low seat. "I think you are about right. I mean," in hasty explanation, "that my dear London that I love is getting near its least lovable stage, and you will be well out of it; you set off the day after to-morrow?"

"Yes."

"Quite alone?"

The tinge of almost caressing pity in his voice goes near upsetting her.

"There is nothing new in that; I have done it before."

"And where are you going?"

"I do not know; I have no fixed plans. I shall make and modify them as I go along."

"You are perfectly right; that is the way to enjoy one's self really."

She is silent. The word "enjoy," though she intends honestly to try and learn what it means by-and-bye, seems at present to have little connection with her dreary, solitary flight from herself.

"And when"—very, almost too kindly— "are we to welcome you back?"

She shakes her head.

"I do not know that, either ; at all events"
—taking the bull by the horns and smiling—
"on my return I shall find you Benedick, the
married man."

He smiles too, but rather anxiously.

"I suppose so."

"Since you have nothing to wait for, I
conclude you will be married as soon as the
season is over ?"

His last answer had come slowly and pen-
sively, but there is energy enough in his next.

"No ; oh dear no! Quite impossible! I
must go to Karlsbad. I cannot risk a repetition of my wretched crippled state. I do
not want the poor child to start in life as a
sick-nurse."

"It will not be till autumn, then ?"

"Autumn!" — he repeats slowly — "yes,
that will be the right season ; gray hairs and
falling leaves go well together."   .

Something in his tone makes her uncomfortable.

"And the *opus magnum*, the "Ἔως ?"

His eye, slightly overcast hitherto, lights up brilliantly.

"She is an ideal sitter. So quick to catch the exact pose I want, and so untiring in keeping it, poor little girl! I am sure that over and over again she must have been ready to drop with fatigue ; when I am in the heat of my work I know how inconsiderate I am. But she has never uttered a murmur."

"The labour we delight in physics pain," replies Anne, ashamed of herself for the bitterness of her quotation, and yet with no more original commentary rising to her lips.

"I suppose" — hesitatingly — "that you would not have time to look in at the studio to-morrow and give your verdict ?"

She turns away her head quickly, with a mixed feeling of sharp pain and self-congratulation. After all he must have very little idea what "looking in at the studio" under these altered circumstances means to her, or he would never have made the proposition.

"No, I think I will wait till—till I come back—till it is finished."

He sighs. " Then you will never see the old place again ?"

" Why not ?"—startled.

" I am going to give it up; in my—my altered circumstances—I must have a house with a studio attached."

" Will not you be sorry to leave it ?"

He seems to feel the stupidity of the question almost as strongly as she does herself, the moment it is uttered.

" Sorry !"—he repeats with asperity, then calming himself—" well, yes, it will be a little bit of a wrench after five-and-twenty years !"

Mrs. Bligh is sympathetically silent ; then she asks :

" You have not begun to look for a house yet, I suppose ?"

" How could I ?"—almost impatiently—" when have I time for anything ? and I cannot "—snipping impatiently with Anne's scissors at the woolly tassel of a sofa-cushion near him—" I cannot get her to say what she would like. I wish that people would say what they like."

CHAPTER XVI.

Mrs. BLIGH had never meant her foreign
trip to be a short one, but it prolongs itself
even beyond her original intention. She
makes her way to the Engadine, where,
thanks to her early start, she is ahead of the
mob of tourists ; and when the greatest heats
are over, drops down into Italy for the vintage. From one high-perched, sweet-named
Italian town to another she wanders, as the
spirit, the guide-book, or the advice of some
chance met or made acquaintance impels her.
The endless succession of new scenes and
objects inevitably diverts her attention from
herself ; and she is too intelligent in mind,
and too sound in body, not—as the calming
and healing weeks go by—to draw from the

old historic sites and older natural lovelinesses of the civilized world's pet and darling much of that enjoyment at whose very name she had mocked at the time of her gloomy setting off. She recovers her flesh and her sleep, and here and there makes a pleasant friend or two.

But from the thought of a return home her soul for several months turns away with dread and aversion. Return to her means an empty little house, the neighbourhood of the friends whom, despite her mental convalescence, she still feels that it will be safer, and at the same time most difficult to avoid ; means manufactured interests and uncongenial work. Her communications with England have been few and slight. Her correspondents — never numerous — have, from the very nature of her travels — so entirely planless and guided by the impulse of the moment — been baffled in their efforts to keep in touch with her. She has had, indeed, several letters from Mrs. Mulholland, conscientiously covering every inch of very thin

paper, full of trifling family details, and
running over with alternate ecstasies and
lamentations over the beauty, commodity and
ironical too-bigness of George's new house.
From Pamela she has received a few short
notes, each of which she has laid down with
a balked sense of how unsatisfactory a scribe
Miss Capel-Smith has become. Not one of
her dull and superficial billets gives an explanation of the fact that she is still Miss
Capel-Smith.

It is, perhaps, under the circumstances,
natural enough that her mentions of her
betrothed are so few and sketchy. He has
gone to Karlsbad. He has come back.
They have been looking at houses together.
The latter fact—out of regard, no doubt, to
her friend's feelings—in a rather indistinct
postscript. Before the end of November
even these baffling scraps of information
have ceased to reach her; and Pamela is
altogether dumb. Mrs. Bligh explains this
silence to herself in her own way.

The marriage—already delayed beyond

her expectations—has at length taken place. Pamela is on her honeymoon. There is nothing surprising in her letting that period pass without making Anne a sharer in its joys, but the latter feels a prick of pained annoyance that the wedded pair should have thought it kinder not to impart to her the date of their union. It is true that she has seen no announcement of the event in the English papers ; but since she has read them with no regularity, she may easily have missed the particular issue in which it appeared.

It is not till the week before Christmas that she sees again her native shores ; to which she returns with her mind about as dark as the wintry weather around her concerning those two of her country - people whose doings chiefly interest her. She reaches home late and fagged, after a through journey from Turin, and a sick and stormy crossing. She goes to bed almost at once, thankful to the bodily fatigue which blunts the sense of dreariness of her unwelcomed home-coming. It comes up with and overtakes her next morning, however, when she wakes up to the consciousness of being boxed in by a close and dirty darkness of ill-smelling fog.

"What possessed me to come home?" she ejaculates to herself, over her murky, gas-lit breakfast; to *herself*, since as yet she has not even the dogs to make her moan to—"*home* indeed!" In the afternoon the filthy ebony veil lifts a little, and she goes out shopping. It is odious out of doors, but anything is better than to sit at home, a prey to the vain and melancholy memories that, despite her changed and braced condition of being, throng back upon her in the depression of the heavy atmosphere, where dirt has taken the place of light.

The shops are crowded to suffocation with people buying Christmas presents. She can scarcely make her way through the eager throngs, or gain any hearing from the distracted shopmen and women for her modest requirements. She is standing near the door of a pretty shop in Oxford Street, waiting for the chance of an opening, and making the reflection which must occur over and over again to us all—even though not like Mrs. Bligh, just returned from the leisurely elbow-room of a happier and emptier clime— how hideously thick we are upon the ground, when the sound of a familiar voice, uplifted in the intense exasperation of a mild-tempered person whose patience is at an end, salutes her ears.

"May I ask?" inquires Mrs. Mulholland, making a frenzied clutch at a heated shop-boy who is hurrying past her, "is there any chance of my *ever* being served? I have been waiting here five-and-thirty minutes, and as my time is extremely limited—— *Nan!*"

In the joyful surprise of catching sight of her friend, Mrs. Mulholland lets the relieved *employé* slip through her fingers, while she and her daughters push their way with a vigour before which all impediments yield, to the spot where Anne is standing.

" Well, this *is* nice!"—kissing her warmly —despite the publicity of the place—" I had not an idea you were back."

" I only arrived last night."

" Well, I suppose you have been seeing all kinds of fine places.   You will think us poor stay-at-homes very humdrum."

" How well she is looking!" cries Lucile. " I declare, Anne, that you have got a sort of foreign cut about you."

" Have I ?"—grateful for and warmed by the kindly looks of the three simple, affection-ate faces round her—yet a little embarrassed by their unanimity of scrutiny; "and you all ? You do not look as if much ailed *you.*"

" Oh, we are in great form, thank God! You should see Czar. He is looking so ridiculously young; you have only just missed him; we have had such difficulty in getting him out of the shop; we wanted him out of the way because we have clubbed together to buy a really good Christmas surprise for him."

"We have been staying with George at his new house," says Sue, triumphantly getting her oar in for the first time; "it is such a beautiful house—such lots of room it it. I dare say he will ask you to stay with him. He can put us all up, and all the dogs and both the donkeys, too!"

"Indeed!" with a transient inward flash of compassion for the lonely-hearted George, mocked by the spacious emptiness of his abode.

"He is going to spend Christmas with us at Plas Drow," says Lucile; "we are all going down together to-morrow; we mean to have such fun in the train. George is going to pretend to have mumps, to keep people out of the carriage."

This last piece of information inspires Mrs. Bligh with a surprised doubt as to whether the pity she had been lavishing upon Miss Capel-Smith's rejected lover is not a little superfluous.

"It will be *diagonally* opposite to George's last visit to us, when he moped so dreadfully!" almost shouts Sue, in her joyful excitement.

" Pamela is coming down with us too."

" Pamela!" repeats Anne, in a tone of intense surprise; "then when is the wedding to be?"

Her three hearers look at each other with a puzzled air, then break into a simultaneous laugh.

" We do not say anything about that yet awhile," answers Mrs. Mulholland, nodding sagely; "of course, such an idea has never been mooted by anyone as yet. It would be scarcely decent."

" *Scarcely decent?*"

" Why, yes, it would be rather a case of ' One down, t'other come on '; it is scarcely three weeks—is it, girls?—since her engagement was broken off."

" *Broken off! Her engagement!*" Anne can get out nothing but these fragmentary repetitions, and even they come gaspingly. " Do you mean to say——"

She breaks off.

They are looking at her paled and quivering face with a new light of astonished comprehension on their features.

"And do you mean to say that you do not know— that you have not heard that it *is* broken off?"

She shakes her head, incapable of speech, uncertain whether she wakes or sleeps.

"We thought, of course, that she had told you."

"She—she did not know where I was exactly—I was moving about; but"—her senses coming slowly back to her, accompanied by a passionate anxiety for the details of the astounding, and as yet all unrealizable, event "please tell me—I know nothing— how did it come about? Was it her doing or—or *his?*"

"I do not think I ever quite made out," replies Mrs. Mulholland, still surveying, with a rather astonished air, the extraordinary change in her friend's complexion—"did you, Luce? I think it was a case of mutual consent. For my part, I always thought it a silly sort of affair; even if there had been no George in the case, I should have said just the same. I never could understand what she saw in him—no, girls, do not talk nonsense; it had nothing to say to his age. No doubt he is a very good sculptor, and, from what you told us of him, he is certainly a very expensive one; but when it comes to marrying——"

It seems to Anne as if she should never be able to disentangle herself from the questions, the comments, the endearments of her companions in order to carry out a plan which she is passionately anxious to put in action without a moment's delay. When at length—it costs her conscience a wading knee-deep in lies to effect it—she has freed herself from them, she jumps into the first hansom, without a glance either at the wheel-tires, or the horse's knees, and has herself driven to the house of Miss Capel-Smith, whose presence in London she has learned from the Mulhollands. As she goes along, she asks herself how she shall possibly bear the delay if she is met by a "not at home."

But this *contretemps* is spared her; Miss Capel-Smith is at home, and as her parents are neither very intimate with, nor very congenial to, Mrs. Bligh, the latter has no scruple in having herself shown directly up to the daughter of the house's high-perched sitting-room. Pamela is stretched in a wicker-chair before a very good fire, with a book in her hand, which, on the visitor's entrance, is ruthlessly tumbled on the floor, while the hand and arm that supported it are with its fellow flung round Anne's neck.

" You darling woman! I *am* glad to see you!"

The manner is an obvious return to the earlier and adoring one, but Mrs. Bligh pushes her restored worshipper gently but decidedly away, looking piercingly at her the while. The girl's beaming eyes drop a little.

" I—I see that you have heard. Are you ——are you *very* angry with me?"

Perhaps it is only Anne's guilty fancy that there is a slight but mirthful tremble at the corners of Pamela's mouth as she puts the deprecating question.

" Have you thrown him over?" she asks sternly.

The lovely culprit's eyes still droop; for a moment she hesitates, then breaks into an uncontrollable fit of laughter.

" Do not kill me for laughing!" she says indistinctly. " But if you only knew—there is such a ludicrous contrast between your tragic face and the facts of the case! I threw him over! Yes, I threw him over ; but, oh, how thankful he was to be thrown!"

" What?"

" He was far too chivalrous ever to have done it himself; but, oh, he *was* obliged to me!"

Anne is silent, staring at her young companion with a feeling of stupefaction, behind and through which some enormous muffled joy seems to be stirring.

" Let us talk comfortably," says Pamela,

putting her softly into the wicker chair, and
lying down on the rug at her feet. " You
really need not look at me like a tigress
robbed of her whelps ; I am a *great benefac-
tress* to him ; ask him "—laughing delightedly
again—" if I am not."

Anne is still too stunned, and with everything too much in a whirl about her to make
any comment. Only her eyes, into which
the light of a great yet doubting joy is
coming, ask for further explanation of this
bewildering riddle.

" Well, you see," pursues Pamela, leaning
her silky rust-coloured head against her
friend's knees, " when the sittings were done
—he really *has* made a wonderfully beautiful
thing of me—he went to Karlsbad and I
went to stay with Lady ——"

" That is where George Mulholland is
sub-agent, is not it ?"

" Ye—es, I believe so ; that is neither
here nor there !"—impatiently—" and when
he came back from Karlsbad—it had brought

on his gout and made him very cross—and
I came back from ——"

"Yes?"

"He naturally had to dance attendance a
good deal upon me. I had to take him
about and introduce him to my friends; and
it broke into his work a good deal; you
know what a passion he has for his work,
and how he feels towards interrupters of
it?"

"Yes, I know."

"But what finished him—what finished us
both, I think, was looking at houses together; we went over five mansions in
Belgravia and three in South Kensington
from basement to attic, and on the morning
after the eighth I sent for him and told him
that I thought we should be happier apart.
You should have seen his face; the unsup-
pressible rapture of relief struggling through
his honest endeavours to look broken-
hearted!" She stops to laugh softly again.
Then turning round so as to place her elbow
on Anne's knees, and lift the dewy rosy

gaiety of her face towards hers. "You dear
thing, what possessed you to put it into our
heads that we were in love with each other?
He is an Admirable Crichton as far as delightfulness goes, but he *is* a little old! We
are, thank God, *quitte pour la peur*, but
we really must insist"—with a charming
wheedling gesture—"upon your giving up
match-making!"

    *   *   *   *   *

The fog settles down thick again upon
London as the night draws on, and Mrs.
Bligh's house is as full of it as suffocated
little house can be; but to its owner it
seems to be alight with the sunshine of India
or Egypt. Nor is the inky vapour thick
enough to hinder one who feels his way
along the little street towards tea-time, and,
after groping awhile, finds the electric-bell.
His beautiful gray frock-coat is exchanged
for a wintry tweed, suited to the austerity of
the season; and he has no Malmaison; but
there is not a touch of winter in his look, as
he draws the *pouf*—she remembers how he

had eschewed it on his last visit—to her feet, and says with a long, low sigh of content, " Dear little friend, how pleasant it is to be here again !"

THE END.